# Legasea

## Krystalyn Drown

A Division of **Whampa, LLC**
P.O. Box 2540
Dulles, VA 20101
Tel/Fax: 800-998-2509
http://curiosityquills.com

© 2013 Krystalyn Drown

ISBN: 978-1-62007-162-5 (ebook)
ISBN: 978-1-62007-163-2 (paperback)
ISBN: 978-1-62007-164-9 (hardcover)

# Table of Contents

*For Serena,*

*who has read everything I've ever written*

# Chapter One

The moment I stepped onto the boat, I was breaking my mom's number one rule: Never go into the water without parental supervision. But that rule was ancient. Would one tiny crack even be noticed?

And more importantly, could a party on a hundred foot yacht be considered breaking the rule? It was more like a party on a private island. *Safe as houses*, my grandma would say. Although my mom would say I was begging for trouble.

Ian stood on the boat with his arm stretched out to me. Mae dug her sharp elbow into my ribs, nudging me toward him. "Come on, Aye. No one's gonna see you out there."

I peered down the dock through the endless tangle of fishing boats, every one of them locked up for the night. The boat in front of me was the only one with any sign of life. No one was around to spot me. No one would tell my mom. Even the moon complied by sliding behind a dark cloud.

I still didn't move.

As if sensing my reluctance, the water sent out its own plea. The waves rocked the boat. The gentle up and down motion beckoned me closer. I could play it safe and go home like a good little girl, or I could listen to my body and the way every nerve buzzed at the first scent of briny air.

I felt myself rising onto the balls of my feet, ready to jump in, then I stopped myself by lowering my heels and curling up my toes.

"Aileen?" Mae jiggled my arm.

"What? Oh." While I stood there being the indecisive queen of the world, everyone else had climbed on board. Kids were plunking drinks into coolers, seeking out private places to . . . ya know, and untying the ropes so they could cast off.

Mae would never let the party leave without her. Thirty more seconds and she would get everyone to join in a rousing chorus of "Come on, Eileen," a song she'd learned from my dad. Sure enough, she threw her arm over my shoulder and leaned in toward my ear, giggling and humming at the same time.

She sang quietly at first, then her voice grew louder while a few other kids picked up the tune.

The lapping waves joined in with their sweet siren song, the one that had serenaded me my entire life. No matter how much I longed for the water, it was always just beyond my reach. It had been years since the accident, yet my mom held on to the past like a stubborn child.

"You coming?" Ian's hand waited for me. His gray eyes sparkled with a hint of mischief, a look I once knew very well, and I wondered what he had planned for the night. While hanging out with him didn't thrill me, I couldn't help but feel everyone's excitement charging through the air. The last party he and his brother, Stephen, had thrown lasted for two days and involved a trapeze, two dozen bubble machines, and a goat.

"Pretty, pretty pleeeease," Mae giggled into my ear. Her dark curls sprang up and down as she bounced at my side. "You've been talking about this party all week. You can't chicken out now."

And I'd hate myself if I did. Obviously, Mom would never let me go, but since I was spending the night at Mae's and *her* parents had approved, I technically had permission. Who knew when I'd have another chance to go out on the water?

"Oh, what the hell." If my mom was going to kill me, at least my last night would be spent in luxury. Ignoring Ian's hand, I jumped onto the pristine white deck as a silly grin spread across my face.

"That's my girl," Mae said, grabbing my shoulders and landing with a thunk behind me.

Steven shouted out, "Let's do it," as he headed toward the helm. When he looked back over his shoulder and added, "Good to see you, Mae," she giggled.

"Have fun, ladies." Ian flashed a sly grin as he followed his brother. Within moments, the motor purred to life, churning the water beneath us, and setting us free. From land, rules, and everything.

Mae took off on a mission to stalk Steven, her crush since, well, last Monday when she'd heard about the party. Because of the boat's size, it wasn't long before I lost track of her. There were three levels. The bottom two were enclosed and filled with food tables and pounding music. The top level was an open deck and even had a hot tub. A few couples wandered around outside and disappeared into the shadows, but most people either went inside or to the top. I had never ridden on anything so ritzy, and if it had been tied up at the docks, I would have loved to explore. But as this was my first journey into the bay in thirteen years, I followed my instinct.

The star-filled night turned the bay into something vast and infinite, an unknown territory waiting to be explored. I dug through a cooler, passing up the fruity drinks and beers for a 7up and took my place by the port railing.

As we sailed away from the dock, our tiny stretch of Oregon coast grew smaller. The dock lights shone like ghosts, a slight mist hovering around them, waiting to guide us home when the time came. I hoped it never did. Judging by the music and laughter I heard coming from inside, everyone on board felt the same. It was quiet where I stood though, just the purr of the motor and whoosh of the water.

Off in the distance, the black outlines of dozens of rock islands dotted the bay, like shadow puppets posing in front of the star-filled sky. I tried to memorize them all so I could paint them later. A gentle spring breeze tossed my hair and warmed my skin. I reached over the side, feeling the salt spray tickle my hand.

About ten feet away, a seal poked its head above water and looked around, his movements agitated. I recognized him as one of the seals that hung out on the beach behind my house.

"What's wrong?" I asked.

His eyes met mine, and he let out a low, purposeful growl that felt very much like a warning. When he ducked under and raced off, an uncomfortable feeling curled up inside my chest. I'd watched the seals in the bay my entire life, and I'd never seen one react like that. A moment later, three more streaked through the water in their race to get away.

From what? I could only think of one thing.

Against all common sense, I leaned over the edge. The moon disappeared again, darkening the water into a black void. My heart hammered its protest against my ribs as I searched for the threat. *Please don't be a shark. Please don't leap out and—*

"Having fun?"

I jumped, and a small cry escaped my lips. Ian appeared from around the corner, a million watt grin on his face. It disappeared though when he saw me clutching my chest and realized he'd scared the snot out of me.

"I'm sorry," he said. "Are you okay?"

I cast my eyes out to the water, feeling stupid for letting myself get freaked out by the seals. "Yeah, I'm fine." It was probably my own guilt for being out there in the first place. It would have been too embarrassing to explain that to him though. The guilt part. Not the broken rule. He was well-versed on those.

"Good." Ian planted himself beside me, his eyes focused on the horizon just like mine. A silent moment passed, and I wondered why he was with me instead of inside, flirting with some freshman. Ian and I had been friends as kids, but middle school had brought an end to that. "So, what do you think—?"

The boat lurched, and the world dropped into slow motion.

I lost my balance and slammed into the railing. The top part of my body tilted over the edge, and in my mind, I realized my mom was right. This was a very bad idea. But my body told my mind to shut up. As my fingers grazed the water, a shock went up my arms and sent tingles along my skin. I had come into the bay for a reason, and it wasn't because I wanted to ride in a boat. Every inch of me longed to know what it felt like to be completely surrounded by water.

As if sensing my curiosity, the waves reached up to me, wrapping themselves around my arms and pulling me forward. Reality didn't set in until I sucked in that first lungful of salt water. And with reality, came panic.

Water. Me. Drowning. Bad, bad idea.

The world snapped back to normal speed as I screamed and flailed, feeling for anything to grab hold of.

Strong arms wrapped around my legs, and despite my kicking, hauled me back into the boat. I landed on trembling legs and clutched at Ian's t-shirt, coughing and gasping. He held tight to my waist while I buried my head into his shoulder and tried not to cry.

"It's okay," he said. "I've got you."

I nodded, unable to speak. I felt like the railing had left a dent in my stomach, but that wasn't what had silenced me. If I had gone over . . . Oh, God. And what scared me even more was that part of me had wanted to be engulfed by the water. It had happened once before, and I knew how badly that turned out.

"Th— thanks." I lifted my head from his shoulder. I should have pulled away right then, but I needed to feel stable for just a moment longer.

"You're welcome." A hunk of blonde hair fell across his forehead, and I remembered how I used to brush it out of his eyes. And how he used to smile when I did it. As if on cue, that perfect smile appeared. "You know, swimming isn't such a bad idea. There's a cove about a mile east. We have some wetsuits downstairs. What do you think?"

*That you had a chance with me in eighth grade, but you cheated on me with Sarah Brewster.*

"Um, no thanks." I eased out of his grasp, but before I got two steps away, the boat lurched again. I grabbed him by the sleeve. "What was that?"

A grinding sound came from the propellers. Ian's head snapped up toward the helm. "Steven, what the hell do you think you're doing?"

I followed his gaze and saw Steven yanking hard on the wheel. "We're caught on something. I don't know what. Let me try to—"

A scream ripped through air, followed by a dozen more, all coming from the back of the boat. Ian and I ran toward the crowd to look down at the propeller. As I pushed through, some girl stumbled backwards, spilling her beer all over my shirt, but neither of us cared. I doubted she even noticed because of what she was backing away from.

Tangled on the blades was a thick rope, and tied up in that rope, was a dead girl floating on her back. I didn't recognize her, but she looked about my age, maybe older. It was hard to tell. She was blue and bloated, and the pain in my stomach turned into heart-pounding nausea. I grabbed hold of the railing, ready to be sick.

"Steven, cut the motor!" Ian shouted over everyone's cries.

"Um . . . Ian." Some guy elbowed him and pointed across the water.

Red and blue lights flashed through the darkness, approaching us with a speed and purpose that turned Ian's already panicked face a ghost white.

"Oh, shit," he said.

"Arrested?" My mom paced the wooden floor in front of the sofa. With each step, the family pictures that lined the wall hammered the gray paneling. Our ancestors watched my humiliation in silence.

I sat in my father's recliner. He leaned against the wall beside me with his arms folded across his chest, his lips sealed just above his sun-bleached beard. He hadn't made a sound since he'd picked me up.

"I wasn't arrested," I said in my tiniest voice, even though it was true. Ian's father had only pressed charges against his sons. The police had released the rest of us to our parents at the docks.

"Oh, really?" My mom pivoted mid-step and stomped toward me. "I received a phone call at one a.m. saying to come pick up my daughter for partying on a stolen boat. What would you call it?"

I shrunk back into the chair. "A mistake? The boys said they had permission."

"And not only that," Mom said, ignoring my excuses, "you were found at the scene of a murder!"

"The police never confirmed it was a murder." Although there was no denying it. No one could tie themselves up like that, not on purpose and certainly not by accident. The ropes were too tight. The knots, too precise.

"So that makes it okay?"

"No, just not our fault." After we'd docked the boat, the police spent two hours questioning us. None of us knew the girl although her face was so bloated I wasn't sure I would have recognized her even if I had seen her around town. I doubted she went to our school though. Gossip about a missing girl would have spread quickly, and that girl looked like she'd been dead for a while. When our parents arrived, the police told them we'd simply been in the wrong place at the wrong time. In a stolen boat.

"What about when you climbed into that boat? Are you innocent of that too?" She planted her feet and put one hand on her hip, cocking her shoulder as she did so. "Did someone kidnap you? Tie you up and toss you in? Because it looks to me like you directly disobeyed our rules."

One stupid rule. "I just wanted to go for a ride," I said quietly.

"And look what happened! What if you were the girl they found floating out there? You can't swim, Aileen!"

"I know."

"Did you forget what happened to your grandfather? What nearly happened to you?"

"No, ma'am." My words got smaller and smaller as I begged the chair to swallow me whole.

"And you were drinking! I can smell it all over you. You're barely sixteen, for God's sake."

"I wasn't drin—"

"I don't even know what to do with you." At that, she turned away, probably to count to twenty before she started yelling again.

I glanced up at my Dad, pleading with him to do his job. To defend me. To make mom laugh. To do *something*.

He moved behind the chair, placing his hands on my shoulders like he did whenever I struggled with a difficult painting. He'd usually press his thumbs into my shoulder blades and rub the tension away while belting out some ridiculous song he learned from his grandparents. He always knew how to make me feel better. Tonight, however, the pressure from his thumbs felt tight and constricting. "You messed up, Aye."

"Damn straight, she did!" Mom flipped back to me, her fury redoubled. "And if you think you're hanging out with that Mae again, you're—"

"None of this is her fault!" I pushed my dad's hands from my shoulders and stood up. If he wasn't going to say anything, I had to. My mom didn't care about the boat, the girl, the alcohol, or even who I hung out with, so much as her stupid rule. "If it's so important for you to keep me away from the water, then why don't we move? I hear Kansas is ocean free."

Mom narrowed her eyes and said very slowly, "You know we can't."

"Why not? I can't drown in a tornado."

"Aileen Kathryn Shay, if you don't cut that sass—"

"Enough!" Grandma Fee commanded from the doorway. In the second it took to focus on her, she had maneuvered her wheelchair past the couch and straight to the center of the room. As a girl, she'd been exotic-looking with long, brown hair and huge, brown eyes. With her beauty and physical presence, she could command any room. But even now, dressed in her long, white nightgown, her gray braid wrapped around her head, and sleep crusting her eyes, we couldn't take our eyes off her.

My mother's posture softened instantly. "Mom, I'm sorry. I didn't mean to wake you. Why don't you go back to bed and we'll—"

"Ciara, stop it," Fee said in an even voice. "It's late. Let the child go to bed. She'll still be here in the morning, but your anger won't."

The glint in the corner of my mom's eye said she wanted to argue. But no one argued with Fee. With great reluctance, Mom turned to me and said, "Go to your room. We'll discuss your punishment tomorrow. Plan on at least a month."

Without a word, I slid past Fee, patting her shoulder on my way out. She grabbed my fingers and gave them a squeeze, a touch far more reassuring than my dad's. Why couldn't she have lived with us during all those summers I'd begged to take swimming lessons with Mae? I bet she would have stuck up for me, instead of carting me off to art classes at the community center. It's not that I didn't love drawing. There was just something I loved more.

In my bedroom, I popped off my shoes, climbed onto my window seat, and pressed my forehead against the cool glass. The moon was high and bright. I could see its reflection sparkling on the ocean, hear the water shifting back and forth over the sand. Our wooden pier jutted out about fifty feet; the pilings at the end stood abandoned and lonely, our boat sold to some stranger thirteen years ago. I remembered it though, white with a red stripe, *Sea Spirit* painted on the side. On clear nights, I imagined its ghost lingering there, promising me the entire ocean if only I'd ask.

Was Mom ever going to stop being afraid? It was a freak accident. One I barely remembered, but she refused to forget.

Too restless for sleep, I slid my window open and jumped through, landing on the soft sand below. From there, it was only a short walk over a narrow strip of grassy dunes, past the knotted stump, and down the beach to my rocks.

The closest of the large weather-beaten rocks rested right along the water line. The other one jutted up through the water about ten feet out and ten feet to the left. And in the shallows curving between the two, a low, flat bridge of rock connected them, almost like the three rocks had once been teeth, and the middle one had broken off. Even at high tide, the water on one side only reached ankle deep, but if I lay across the bridge on my stomach and stretched out over the other side, I could swirl my arms in the deeper water. I liked to pretend I was floating on the ocean, listening to the birds and the barking of nearby seals.

My mom would have a freak attack if she saw me doing it, but it was far enough from the house, and shielded by enough grass and rocks that she couldn't see me. And I only did it when I absolutely needed to. When the call of the water got too strong, or my parents' rules grew too thick. Otherwise, I played nice and pretended I didn't care, pretended there wasn't some huge, gaping hole inside my gut that terrified me, and fascinated me, and made me think crazy thoughts when the ocean tried to claim me as its own.

As I lay there, dipping my fingers in the soft, starlit waves, the tears fell. One, two, three, four, five, six, seven . . .

"Hey," a voice called out from behind me. "Whatcha doing?"

# Chapter Two

I pushed myself into a sitting position. The new boy from next door was standing before me. Well, it wasn't technically next door, but it was the only other house on our stretch of the beach, so even though they lived about four or five blocks away, they were our only neighbors. And complete strangers.

Neither he nor his sister had ever showed up at school, and no one knew much about them other than what groceries they bought at the Pack 'n Save. We all knew they were fishers because they had a deal with Bill's Seafood Shack, but they didn't have a boat or sign at the marina, and they didn't advertise their business on the bulletin board at my dad's bait shop. In fact, the only boat they seemed to own was a small rowboat tied to the crumbling pier behind their house. They used it nearly every night, but how they used it to catch such a large amount of fish was anybody's guess.

In the three weeks since they'd moved in, I'd seen him come and go, but had never gotten a close-up look. Now that I had the opportunity, I couldn't look away. The moon highlighted each feature perfectly. He had dark, shoulder length hair, tanned skin, and *really* nice muscles. He wasn't wearing a shirt, and his bathing suit sat low enough that I could appreciate those lines that well-toned guys get just inside their hips. What he was doing swimming at two a.m. was beyond me, yet here he was, water dripping from his hair, landing on his shoulders and sliding down his . . . wow.

My eyes must have bugged out, because he plopped down beside me, forcing me to look him in the eye.

"I'm Jamie," he said. He had the largest brown eyes I'd ever seen, darker and more fathomless than Fee's. A person could get lost in them.

"I'm, um . . ." *Please don't let him see me blush. Please don't let him see me blush.* "Aileen."

"What's wrong?" He pointed to just under my eye where a tear or two dotted my cheek.

I scrunched my shoulders up and dropped my chin, so my hair covered my face. "Stupid stuff," I said, because I felt stupid that he'd caught me crying. And because the real answer, "My parents don't understand me," seemed trite.

I didn't hear anything for a while. I thought maybe he'd left, but when I straightened up and tucked my hair behind my ears, he was swishing his feet lazily in the water. The dinoflagellates created a soft blue glow around his ankles. When he noticed me looking, he began carving patterns in the water: bioluminescent spirals and triangles, and something faintly resembling a fish.

I stuck my feet in and joined him, flicking my toes in the water and trying to see how far I could send the spray. Of course, I splashed him while I was doing that, and he returned fire. Pretty soon the two of us were laughing and kicking and soaking each other. It was the lightest I'd felt all night. The cold water seeped into my skin and found my soul. It completed me.

Only after there was nothing left to soak, did we call a truce. Exhausted, we lay back on the rock, our faces turned toward each other as our toes dangled in the water. It was warm for a May evening, but with my wet clothes clinging to me and the cool night wind, a tiny shiver ran through me. I barely felt it though. In fact, I couldn't stop smiling.

"The water helps, doesn't it?" said Jamie. "If you've had a bad day."

*It always helps. Bad day or not.* "Is that why you're here?"

He grinned. His teeth formed a crooked line between his lips. "Something like that."

*What do you mean? Why were you out tonight? Did you come to meet me or were you really just swimming?* "That's cool."

He pushed himself to his feet. "It's pretty late. I should go."

I sat up too. *Jamie . . . wait . . .* "Okay. I'll see you around."

"See ya," he said, splashing off.

"When?" I said, surprising myself that I'd said it out loud.

He turned, spread his arms out wide, and grinned. An invitation or a shrug? Then he took off again.

I flopped back on my elbows and huffed. *Alrighty then.*

". . . and up she rises. Way hey and up she rises. Way hey and up she rises ear-lie in tha mornin'." My dad's booming voice carried down the hallway and into my ears.

I buried myself in my comforter. I knew which lyrics came next.

"What do ya do with a drunken' sailor? What do ya do with a drunken' sailor?" My door creaked open and his voice bounced around my tiny bedroom. "What do ya do with a drunken' sailor ear-lie in tha mornin'?"

"Dad, I wasn't drinking." I pushed back my covers to see his weather-beaten smile beaming down at me. In his arms, he held my metal Barney tray, filled with pancakes and 7up. The true loves of my life. Well, except for Barney. We broke up when I was five.

"I know, honey." He placed the tray over my lap and sat down beside me. "After seventeen years as a sailor, I know what drunk looks like. And you weren't it."

"Did you tell Mom that?" I picked up my fork and dug in to my breakfast. No matter how crappy of a night it had been, Dad's pancakes were not to be wasted. Not by me, at least.

"She knows. After you went to bed last night, Fee and I got your sentence reduced to two weeks."

Well, that was good at least. Speaking of . . . "Where is Mom?"

"Pack 'n Save called."

"Ah. The glamorous life of a grocery store cashier."

"Ain't it grand?" But the enthusiasm had gone out of his voice. Little worry lines crinkled beside his eyes, and he looked like he had when I was seven and he told me my pet frog died.

"So what's the bad news?"

"Weeell." Dad patted my knee. "I'm afraid your life isn't going to be too glamorous today either. Mom says since you're grounded, you have to hang out with me at Fish Tales."

And that would explain the pancakes and 7up. I should have seen it coming. Mom's punishments always involved manual labor. I didn't know why Dad thought he needed to bribe me though. What sixteen-year-old girl wouldn't love spending her Saturday at her dad's store scooping worms and squid into Chinese food containers?

Oh wait. Me.

But there was no need for him to feel bad about it. "It's all right," I said, as I polished off my food. "I need to restock my inventory anyway."

"That's my trouper." He chucked me on the shoulder, and the worry lines erased.

Dad pulled our peeling blue pick-up truck to a stop in the alley beside Fish Tales. We couldn't park out front because Old Bertha's smell alone would send the tourists running. She smelled like she'd spent the past thirteen years buried under piles of rotten fish, when in reality, she'd spent it parked by our dumpster, which was sort of the same thing. Luckily my side of the store didn't smell like that or I'd never sell a single painting.

Half bait and tackle/half tourist shop, the fishy part was separated from the rest by a sliding glass door Dad insisted remained closed at all times. He made sure of it by taping a yellow piece of paper to the door, with his message inked in red Sharpie. But just in case Dad's sign didn't catch all the evil-doers, I made a deal for pet odor candles with the pet shop next door. I painted dog and cat pictures for them, and they gave me my fill of candles which kept the tourist side smelling like strawberries, closed door or not.

Today, I pulled nine seal paintings from the bed of the truck, protected of course in triple strength garbage bags, and hauled them into the store. I could paint just about anything—seascapes, lighthouses, boats—but for some reason, the tourists liked the seal paintings. If they spotted one on the beach, they wanted a memento of that experience. And if that's what they wanted, I was happy to provide it in exchange for a donation to my car and clothing fund. Well, scalping was more like it considering what I paid for the canvas and paint, but if they were willing to pay it, I was willing to take it.

After I had arranged and priced all of my things, I headed over to the fishy side, threw on a thick, vinyl apron and got to work filling bait containers. A few local fishermen had daily orders with us, although their numbers had cut in half in the last year or so. It was a good thing we also catered to the tourists who wandered up and down the pier with fishing poles, whooping with joy every time they caught a smelt. I didn't have the heart to tell them they could have bought some from us and saved themselves the trouble.

Mont, once my dad's fishing buddy, now his part-time assistant, showed up soon after. He nodded toward my new additions on the tourist side. "Got some purty pictures in there."

"Thanks," I said as I scooped up a slimy load of worms.

"You're staying away from them selkies, right? I've heard tell of some making appearances round these waters."

He walked with a bit of a limp, spoke with a bit of a drawl, and talked with a bit of a lie. As far as I knew, he'd never traveled farther east than his shack by the dock, and most of his stories came from the books on sea legends we sold to the tourists. But he made me smile, nonetheless.

"I'll stay on the lookout." I assured him.

"You best do that. They's slippery little things." He lifted a crooked finger and tapped his right knee. "I got the bad joints to prove it."

"Oh, really?" It was an old joke between us. There wasn't a legend out there that wasn't responsible for some scar on his body. That particular story involved an underwater cavern and several weeks' capture as the selkies interrogated him and repeatedly bit him in order to learn the whereabouts of a captured maiden. I'd seen the bite marks on his leg and was willing to bet he'd simply pissed off the wrong dog. He always seemed to own at least a couple.

"Come on, Mont. You know better than to look for a selkie as a girlfriend. You may steal her skin and take her for your own, but the moment she finds where it's hidden, she'll go back to the sea."

"Don't I know it." He patted my shoulder and shuffled to the counter to ring up an order.

Just as I was closing out the cash register for the evening, the bell over the door jingled.

"I'm sorry. We're—" But I stopped when I saw who was standing there . . . the stupid ass who'd been hounding my dad about selling the store. His name was Ben something-or-other, and he was stocky, wearing a slick, gray suit that probably cost more than our truck. Yet he was offering a quarter of what the property was worth, and when that ran out what would we do? Live off Mom's cashier income for the rest of our lives? Besides, this shop was my dad's everything, his only contact with the life that had ended with the accident. "We're closed," I said with a firm voice and a hard look.

"For how long?" Ben tilted his head and widened his eyes with feigned innocence.

"Just overnight," I said, pretending I hadn't noticed his real meaning.

"Riiight." He filled the extra syllables with doubt and stepped through the doorway, knowing I wouldn't kick him out. Dad had told me to humor him whenever he came by. Apparently, that man had dated my mom in high school. Then, he went away to college, returning a couple of months ago with more money than Midas, wanting to invest in the town he'd grown up in. And by "invest," he meant demolish our way of life. Each time I saw that smug expression on his face, it became harder and harder to keep my mouth shut.

He strolled around the store, scribbling notes in a notebook, smelling the bait in the cooler, and bending down the tips of fishing poles and frowning. I followed him, glaring any time he touched our stuff and turning red with embarrassment when he noticed the dust on some of our shelves. True, things hadn't been selling as well as they should, but that didn't give him the right to act like he owned the place.

When he got to the door leading to the tourist side, he stopped and stared at my seal paintings. His hungry look creeped me out, like a circling shark waiting to close in for the kill.

"Nice work," he said, though it was hard to tell if he was being sincere.

"Thanks," I said, assuming he wasn't. "Are you gonna buy one?"

His answer came in the form of a shrug, a casual movement that made me wish I could growl at him. He headed toward the front door, but paused at our bulletin board. "You won't mind if I post my flyer here? I see you advertise for other businesses." He gestured vaguely at the ads for fishing charters and marine wildlife expeditions. "I'm sure you'd like to alert your customers to the exciting changes coming in the neighborhood." Before I could say no, he selected an orange tack from the bottom of the board and stuck a bright yellow flyer smack into the center, right on top of Mont's ad for weekend fishing trips.

"Thank you so much." He spun on his heel and left the shop.

I stomped over to the board and ripped off the paper. My voice shook as I read the bold, black lettering. "Coming soon. Seal Bay Traders. One store. Two city blocks. No hassle. No fuss. Come shop with us."

I shredded the paper into confetti and buried it in the trashcan under our sandwich wrappers from lunch. He wouldn't take over our street. It would never happen. I knew for a fact the pet store hadn't sold, and the deli did too good business to ever think about selling. There was no way he'd manage to buy up all of Main Street. It wasn't gonna happen. It wasn't.

The office/storage room door creaked open. Dad's head appeared in the crack. "Did I hear someone?"

"No, Dad." I peered out the window at the man sliding into his sleek black Lexus. He wore a look of confidence, of triumph. I imagined smacking that look off his face. "There was no one."

That night, I stayed up until two, watching the beach to see if I spotted anyone. Specifically anyone in a low-riding navy blue bathing suit who had smiled at me and flirted with me, and then run away. I even slid up my window and leaned out, looking down the beach toward his house. It was an old property with wooden siding and a half-rotten porch on the back that overlooked the ocean. Until they moved in, the house had stood vacant, though once a month someone cut the grass, and once a year two men made repairs, just enough to keep it from falling down altogether.

Tonight, I'd seen no one. Not even a light to show someone was home, or coming home. Their boat was gone, as usual, but I was pretty sure it wouldn't fit all four of them. Where did they all go? And then, because it was late and I was tired, I started to think I'd imagined Jamie altogether. Or at the very least, imagined he had wanted to see me again.

Eventually, I fell asleep in the window seat. When I woke in the morning, their boat was tied to the pier. Jamie was back, and so was my common sense. What had I been doing? Waiting for him to knock on my window and invite me for a midnight walk? He hadn't promised me anything. Hell, he hadn't even promised he'd talk to me again. Why had I expected it?

I shook my head free of the clutter, most certainly put there by Mae's influence, and got myself dressed for another fun-filled day at Fish Tales.

# Chapter Three

At lunchtime, Mae stopped by and Dad let me disappear with her. Even though Mom hadn't technically lifted her ban, both Dad and I knew it wouldn't last for long. Mae had earned the "forever" on her BFF status, and Mom knew it as well as I did.

On our first day of kindergarten, Brandy Thomkins cornered me by the swing set and made fun of my thrift store dress. It wasn't like it was grubby or anything; it still had the tags on it when Mom picked it out. Brandy, unfortunately, recognized it as a cast off from her birthday party. A group of kids gathered around us, and she told them her mom marked an x on the tag for donation, even grabbing me by the collar to prove she was right. That's when Mae punched Brandy in the stomach, and instead of laughing at me, everyone laughed at Brandy. Mae and I had been inseparable ever since.

It was a good thing for her our loyalty worked both ways. When she wanted to go see her crush, it was my job to go along as moral support, even though I had no idea how to act around said crush's brother. Since the Sarah Brewster incident, the closest Ian and I had come to an actual conversation was Friday night on the boat. And even that was all an act so he could hit on me. I hope he didn't think I was desperate enough to fall for him again. If so, Mae was going to owe me for this.

We walked the short block to the marina where Ian and Stephen were supposed to be cleaning the dock, the first stop in their three hundred hours of community service, awarded for their grievous act of piracy. Mae couldn't stop jabbering about Stephen's eyes, Stephen's hands, Stephen's spleen. If the party invitation had turned her on to him, the fact he was now a criminal made him irresistible. Hence the trip to deliver her homemade peanut butter and honey sandwiches, and maybe coax the boys into a picnic. I guess she figured if he was going to prison, at least he should be well fed.

As we rounded the corner and the dock came in sight, I saw my thoughts weren't that far from the truth. A police car was parked in the fire lane, while the officers themselves were standing on the dock engaged in a very intense conversation with the boys. If I remembered correctly, they were the same officers who had questioned us the night of the party.

Never one to miss out on gossip, Mae grabbed my hand and yanked me toward a trashcan, but it was too late.

"It's the truth. Ask *her*," Steven said, pointing at Mae. We froze halfway to our hiding spot with our mouths wide open. "She was with me the whole night."

Our cover blown, Mae and I skulked back to the sidewalk. A tall, beefy officer lifted his hand, and with one finger, beckoned us to join them. I doubted it was for a picnic.

"So you were with Steven throughout the entire party?" Tall and beefy (his name tag said Rowe) asked Mae.

"Yes, sir."

"And what about you?" He looked to me. One bushy eyebrow rose, and it seemed like it was asking its own questions. "Can you vouch for Ian?"

"Um . . ." I shifted my feet, getting an inch or two away from the question. I may not have been fond of Ian's dating habits, but that was no reason to get him in trouble with the police. Aside from the occasional wild party, he was harmless. I avoided Rowe's gaze by looking down at the ground.

"It's okay," Ian said to me, then answered the question himself. "No, just part of the time. Before I spotted her, I had been inside."

"And most of the kids were inside?" Rowe pressed.

"Yes. Eating, dancing."

"And then you stepped outside?"

"Yes," he said curtly.

Rowe ran his gaze down the length of their yacht. "That thing's pretty big. Are you saying there's someone who can account for your whereabouts from the time you stepped outside until the time you met Aileen?"

Ian's voice rose in frustration. "Well, maybe not all the time. The people outside were pretty . . . occupied . . . with each other."

Rowe's eyebrow wiggled again, like the needle on a lie detector. Practical and creepy all at the same time. "I figured as much."

With a grumble, Ian stuffed his hands in his pockets.

While Rowe was jotting something down in a small spiral notebook, the second officer addressed us. He was young and pimply and went by the name of Hansel. "Did you spot anything unusual on that boat?"

Mae dropped her food basket and folded her arms across her chest, her patience meter having reached its limit. "What are you really asking us?"

Steven touched her shoulder in warning.

Hansel ticked a list off on his fingers. "Any off-limit areas or compartments? A rope that maybe disappeared later?"

"Rope?" I asked, picturing the girl floating in the water behind the boat, her body swollen in the spaces between the tight bindings. I shivered at the memory.

Hansel took a step toward Ian, isolating him from the rest of us. Ian narrowed his eyes, and I finally realized what the officers had been asking.

"Wait a second." I shook my head in disbelief. Ian may have hit on half the girls in our school, but he never physically hurt anyone. "You don't think he killed her, do you?"

"Of course they do," Ian said with a glare at the two police men. "They're saying I stashed her in the boat earlier in the day, then threw her overboard once we got out into the water. All because the stupid rope the girl was tangled in matched a rope I bought last week."

"Well," Rowe said, "if you could produce that rope and show that you—"

"You mean the rope that was bought at her dad's store?" Ian pointed to me. "The same diameter and weight rope that every fisherman around here uses? While you're at it, why don't you just accuse everyone who's ever shopped there?"

Rowe took a step closer to Ian. His eyebrow straightened into a single harsh line as he bent over, practically spitting into Ian's face. "Jane Doe was wrapped in a newly purchased rope, and in the past two months, only four people have purchased that item from the local fishing store. The others are accounted for. Yours, however," he waved his arms around him pointing out the empty air, "seems to have vanished. The girl in question was found attached to your boat. A boat you had, by your own admission, stolen. And she could not have been in the bay for more than a few hours, otherwise the tide would have taken her out. That said, I'm sure you understand why I'm asking, because even though you had witnesses earlier in the evening, and you have your friend here to vouch for you at the time the body was found, you have no one who can verify your whereabouts or your activities from the time you stepped outside until you spoke with Miss Shay here. Is that correct?"

At the mention of my name, I wanted to melt into the dock. Not only was one of my friends (well, former friend) suspected in a murder case, my dad's store was involved too? What if they went after my dad next?

"Well." Rowe's fingers grazed over the handcuffs at his waist as if he were ready to arrest Ian right then. "Do you have an answer?"

Ian backed up against a piling. "I . . . um . . ."

"You're finished, Rowe!" The voice came from behind me. Mr. Glenn, a six foot something man with perfectly styled salt and pepper hair and a blazing glare approached us. "You've badgered my sons enough this weekend."

"Mr. Glenn." Rowe stepped back and straightened himself, giving Ian some breathing room. Behind Rowe's back, Ian pulled his phone out of his pocket and showed it to me. Apparently, he'd called his dad and put it on speakerphone, so his dad had heard everything. If this had been about anything else, I would have laughed. As it was, I didn't even feel relieved. Ian couldn't have killed that girl. But someone did.

"I have a right to my investigation," Rowe insisted.

"And I have the right to kick you off my property." It was true. Their family owned the entire dock and three of the boats. Mr. Glenn tilted his head. It was the only movement he needed to cause Rowe to shrink a little. "My boys have been adequately punished for the crime they committed. I'd say your job here is done. Now why don't you go yell at some third graders for spitting on the playground?"

Rowe stood firmly in place for about half a second. Then, he grunted what could have been an apology and motioned to Hansel who'd been watching the exchange with wide eyes. The two of them retreated to their car, and Mr. Glenn turned to his sons.

"Lunch break?" he asked, eying the basket by Mae's feet.

"Yes, sir," Steven said.

"Twenty minutes." Their dad nodded once, putting a period on his statement, and left.

We all looked at each other for a long moment until Mae couldn't take it anymore. She picked up her basket and chirped, "Sandwiches?"

Steven took the basket from her and gave her a half-hearted smile. Ian and I just stared.

News of the murder spread through the town like a plague. At school, all anyone talked about was the mystery girl, who she was, who'd killed her. The police hadn't released many details so the speculation ran the gamut from unlucky prostitute to rogue member of a non-existent cult. The president of the sci-fi club even suggested she'd been captured by Bigfoot as a child and raised in the woods. When she'd grown too independent, he had . . . disposed of her. The whole club passed out flyers to go camping/hunting near Rogue River this weekend, although I suspected they'd focus more on drinking and making out than they would on trapping monsters.

Me? I went along with the theory that she'd been killed in some far away city, and the murderer dumped her here as he was passing through on the way to someplace else. It made me sleep better, knowing in our town of five thousand inhabitants, there couldn't possibly be a murderer.

I continued working in the store after school and on weekends. I suspected my grounding was only part of the reason Mom insisted I stay there. Yes, she wanted to know I wasn't running off stealing the Mona Lisa or anything, but another part of her was scared. The police were still conducting their investigation which convinced her that the murderer was lurking in the woods directly across from our house.

And she was certain I was his next victim.

I resisted the urge to tape Bigfoot flyers on her car door and waited for her obsession to pass.

Sometime during my second week of worm scooping, I walked into Fish Tales, and my dad pointed me to the tourist side. "You got a live one," he said. "Go reel him in."

"Ah, fish puns." I nudged him in the arm. "Funny, Dad."

"You love it." He scruffed the top of my head, and I ducked away, giggling as I slipped into the other side of the store.

I came to an abrupt halt when I saw Jamie there, standing beneath my painstakingly lettered sign that read, "Paintings by local artist Aileen Shay." His back was to me, and he was fully dressed in jeans and some tour t-shirt, but there was no mistaking who it was. He held one of my smaller paintings, a close up of a seal's face. His thumbs traced over the thick layers of paint.

"This one's my favorite," Jamie said as I stepped up beside him. "The eyes are mesmerizing."

"Thanks." The hairs on his arm brushed against mine, and I sucked in a breath. He smiled, the sneaky kind that said he liked my reaction. Had he brushed against me on purpose?

He cut me a look out of the corner of his eyes. "You're really talented, you know that?"

"I . . . um . . ." Maybe I was or maybe I wasn't. I hadn't figured that out yet. Just like I hadn't figured out whether he was trying to flirt with me. God, I hoped so. But for lack of anything real to say, I pointed to the picture. "That's Owen."

"Owen?" He refocused on the painting: the dark spots around the seal's eyes that formed a mask, the almost white color of his head, the ancient, knowing look in his gaze. "It fits him."

"I thought so, too." There was another, more personal, reason I painted so many seals. If the ocean called to me, the seals were its messengers. Of course, I never told anyone this. But as I stared at Jamie's strong hands and how gently they held my painting, how the wonder in his eyes told me he saw the seals exactly as I did, I realized I wanted him to know. "During certain times of the year, the rocks on the beach are covered with seals. But they always leave space for me on the lowest rock, like they expect me. Owen was my favorite. His last couple of years, his eyes were covered with cataracts, but I'll never forget the way he looked at me, like I was a member of his pod."

"He's gone now?" Jamie's voice was quiet, respectful.

"Last fall." I cried for two days. He still appeared in at least half my paintings.

"I'm sorry to hear that."

"It's okay," I said. And I meant it, because once I got over the loss, I realized he wasn't really gone. The ocean itself was a living, breathing creature. It changed, yes, but nothing in it ever truly went away. After that, I learned to listen for him when I went out to the rocks. To my surprise, I found him there. Or at least I imagined I did. I didn't dare tell Jamie that. Even I knew which confessions sounded reasonable and which ones sounded crazy.

"Do you want to go out there tonight?" he said. "I bet he'd talk to us if we really listened."

I smiled. Guess I'd found someone with the same brand of insanity.

The afternoon crept by. Mont had the day off, so it was just my dad and me, and he spent most of the time locked in the office. He always did that at the end of the month. He told me he was just being meticulous about the bills. He wanted to make sure he crossed every "t" and dotted every "i." But he never said it with a smile, so I knew he was really searching for new and creative ways to pay the bills. We always made it though, so I had to believe we always would.

We only had one or two customers, so I spent most of the time perched on a stool behind the register with my sketchpad on my knees. I tried planning out some new paintings, but the only drawings that made it onto the paper were ones of Jamie's eyes. Large and soulful, with seascapes and dream images woven into the lines of his irises. They might have sold well if I had the guts to put something like that on display, but what if he came back and recognized them? I felt a blush warming my face and promptly removed the pages, folded them neatly, and tucked them into the inside pocket of my school bag.

Jamie and I met at midnight, two hours past Mom's bedtime, because I still had three days left of that pesky grounding. He wore his bathing suit again, but sadly, he wore the t-shirt as well.

"Want to go for a walk?" he asked nervously, as if I'd say no to anything he asked of me.

"Sure." I wondered if my jitters were as clear as his. It wasn't every day a hot, mysterious boy asked me to go for a midnight stroll. Heck, it wasn't any day. Maybe I'd wake up and find this moment had never happened. Some cruel trick my dream-self had played on me. But then his arm brushed mine, and lightning shot through my body, confirming I was wide awake.

We walked down the beach toward his house. If we'd gone quickly, it would have taken maybe five minutes, but we took our time, pausing every now and then. I'd glance at him just to make sure he was still there, and he'd flash me a smile. I couldn't tell what was in that look. Did he know something? Had he asked about me? The town wasn't that big. Nearly everyone could tell him something about me. Or was he just trying to drive me crazy and make me think he knew something?

Finally, I asked, "What is it?"

He shrugged. "Nothing. I was just trying to figure you out."

*Oh, okay then.* "Well, what do you want to know?"

"What do *you* know?"

"About you? Less and less." I knew the sparkle in the corner of his eyes intrigued me. I knew his arms looked so strong I wanted to touch them. And I knew I wanted to know more.

"Fair enough. Ask me anything." His mouth quirked when he said that, like it was a challenge.

"Okay. Where are you from?"

He jumped in front of me and started walking backwards. "Here and there. Last month we lived in Cannon Beach. Before that we stayed with some family up in Forks, Washington." He held his pointer fingers up by his mouth and made little fangs with them.

I kicked some sand at his bare feet, and he danced out of the way. "Liar."

"Yes," he admitted. "But which part?"

"Well, since I've never actually seen you in full sunlight, I'd say the Forks part has to be true."

He threw his head back and laughed to the stars. "Ah, we've just met, and you already know me so well."

"So surprise me," I challenged him. "Tell me something I don't know."

He stopped for a moment, the laughter replaced with the most serious and intriguing look I'd ever seen on him.

Staring up at him, I felt myself teetering at the brink of his dark, shining eyes, ready to fall into the abyss.

His voice lowered into a smoky whisper that sent my pulse racing through my veins. "Do you really want to be surprised?"

There were layers hidden beneath the question, just as dark and fathomless as his eyes. Did I want to uncover them? "Yes."

His lips parted, and for a brief moment, I thought he was truly going to answer me. But then his face slid back into a carefree grin.

I nearly smacked him for teasing me. Instead, I bit my lip and smiled.

"All right. We'll start with my family." He flipped around and continued walking. I fell into step beside him. "I live with my parents and my older sister, Bridget, who, believe it or not, is a little on the crazy side."

"Nothing like you, huh?"

"Nope, not at all." But he winked, a motion that made me giggle. I stepped a little closer to him, and he acknowledged the movement with a smile. I tucked my hair behind my ears, so I could better see the details of that smile. Watching him made the butterflies in my stomach do jumping jacks.

"What else?" I asked.

"More? Okay, let's see . . . I've never owned a pet, but I've always wanted an iguana, I've been home schooled my entire life, and my favorite movie is *Peter Pan*, because I'd love to learn how to fly."

I couldn't resist. "You know, they have these newfangled things called airplanes . . ."

He threw his arm around me, pulled me against his chest, and rubbed his knuckles against my hair.

"Stop! Stop! Okay, I give!" I doubled over with laughter as he released me, but then it faded as my disappointment kicked in. He'd removed his arm from my shoulder, and I wanted it back. Before I could figure out a way to accomplish that, he continued down the beach.

"Okay, your turn," he called back over his shoulder, that sparkle still in his eyes. "What's your favorite color?"

"Blue," I answered, running to catch up. Was he trying to drive me crazy? "But not crayon blue. The deep, almost black blue of the sky right before the sun sets. What about you?"

"Brown," he responded immediately. "But not the crayon color. The soft color of your eyes, and the way it sets off the gold in your hair." And he'd gone all serious again. Intense enough to make me blush. Did he know what his presence did to me? Was he feeling the same thing?

A cool breeze shot through the night. I moved to put my hands in my pockets, but then I realized if I left them out, he might try to hold my hand. I'd suffer through any amount of cold for that. As if reading my mind, he hooked one of his fingers around one of mine, a single thread of connection that sent lightning through me.

After that, we said little. But I kept stealing glances, to make sure he was there and to memorize him in case he decided to disappear again. I think my favorite feature of his was his hair. Most of it was shoulder-length, but it had ragged edges, like it had been cut with a knife instead of scissors. Enough to make him look just a little bit roguish.

For a brief instant, I imagined us twenty years from now, him sitting on a stool in the middle of a kitchen and me standing behind him, trimming his hair exactly the way he wanted it. And I knew how he wanted it, because I'd been the one cutting it for half our lives.

Just the idea of having that moment with him, of knowing him so well, flooded my body with heat. But just in case he *was* a mind reading vampire, I banished the thought as quickly as it had come.

We had long since passed his house when he pointed to a distant rock poking out of the water. Two seals lounged on it, looking up as we approached. One of them rolled over, creating more space on the rock.

"Come on," Jamie said, tugging me to the edge of the water. "We can ask about Owen."

I planted my feet in the sand. "Are you crazy? The water's freezing."

He didn't even consider my protest. "It's not freezing. And you'll be fine."

"Jamie, I can't." The temperature had just been an excuse. Yes, the water was cold, but it rarely bothered me. It was hard to admit the real reason. "It's like fifty feet out. The water's definitely over my head."

"So?" he said, still tugging me. "You can swim, can't you?"

"Umm . . ." I slipped my fingers out of his and turned away. The one thing I hated about myself . . . No, scratch that. I didn't hate myself. I hated my mom and her stupid obsessions. *Don't go in the water. Don't leave the house without an adult. Don't live your life.* Anger and frustration built up inside me until I felt like I was ready to punch something. Even asleep, Mom was ruining things for me.

Jamie stepped up behind me. His warm hands found their way to my shoulders, and in his effort to soothe me, he discovered the tension that had been building for most of my life.

"I'm sorry. I didn't know. I assumed since you live on the beach—"

"There was an accident." The words slipped out. Except for my family and Mae, no one knew this story. So why was I telling Jamie? The only explanation my mind would give was that he needed to know. "When I was three, we were out in my dad's fishing boat. Me, my parents, my Grandma Fee, and my Grandpa Colm. I don't remember it, but my parents say a storm appeared out of nowhere that knocked me off the boat. Colm jumped in to save me, but the rain was too thick, the wind was too strong. He disappeared, and so did I." I gulped in a breath, because my next memories were so faint, I couldn't be sure if they were real. Everyone told me they were ridiculous, so I'd begun to censor them, even in my own mind. Even now with Jamie, I couldn't bring myself to mention them. "I was gone for three days. Everyone thought I was dead. But then early one morning, Fee walked by herself down to the water's edge and found me alive."

I felt a gentle pressure on my shoulders as Jamie turned me around. I looked up into his eyes. He was wrong. *His* eyes were the perfect shade of brown.

"After that, my mom vowed I would never go out in the water again. The ocean was selfish. She was afraid if it got hold of me again, it wouldn't give me up."

Jamie nodded, as if all of this made perfect sense. Well, he had me beat there, because to me, it made as much sense as an elephant DJ-ing a school dance. Then, he asked a question even crazier than my story. "Do you want to learn to swim?"

*Yes. Yes. A thousand times yes!* "I don't have a swimsuit."

He took one look at my clothes, a fitted t-shirt and capris, and said, "You'll dry. Come on."

This time, I followed. The water was icy, but the heat from his touch made it all worthwhile. Jamie led me out until we were about waist deep. I felt an odd thrill as the water swirled around my body. Up until a couple of weeks ago, I had never defied my mom's rules. No matter how much I complained, I was always afraid there might be some truth in them. Yet here I was, going out in the water for the second time in less than two weeks. And everything about it felt completely right.

"Now lay on your stomach," he said. "I've got you."

I kicked up one leg and was about to kick up the other when something wrapped around my ankle. I screamed and jumped about three feet away. "There's something in the water! A rope! There's someone there!"

Jamie laughed, plunged his hand into the water, and fished around until he came up with what had gotten me—a fistful of seaweed.

My eyes darted around, looking for someone, something other than us. I didn't see anything, but after being subjected to so many of my mom's worries, they had somehow become my own. I ran out of the water, fisting the fear out of my eyes.

Jamie splashed after me, catching up only after we reached the sand. He touched my arm, and I flipped around. "It's okay. It's just a plant. There's tons of it out there."

"No, it's not that," I said. "It's just . . . that murdered girl. I was there when she was found floating in the bay. No one knew who she was, but we—"

"Stop." He grabbed hold of my arms, his body rigid with panic. "What girl? How old? What did she look like?"

"Um . . . straight, dark hair. Pale skin. Maybe sixteen or seventeen. Her picture's been all over the news."

"We don't have a TV." Jamie said it like it was the most disastrous thing in the world, and the way his whole body seemed to shrink up a little, I knew it wasn't because he was upset about missing season twenty-seven of Survivor. His jaw tightened, his shoulders drew in, and he didn't blink for a long time. The distance in his eyes told me he wasn't with me anymore. He was seeing something else. Or someone else, with straight, dark hair and pale skin.

"Do you know who—?"

"I've got to go." And without another word, he took off toward his house.

# Chapter Four

"I think he did it," Mae said the next day between classes.

"Jamie?" I asked. She didn't see me roll my eyes as I dug in my locker for books.

"Or someone in his family." She leaned against a closed locker, her books clutched to her chest while her mind skipped merrily through the fields of lunacy. "Think about it. You said he recognized the girl's description and ran off to tell his family. A family that either hides in their house or goes out who knows where on that little boat. Besides, you're convinced the killer is someone from out of town. They just moved here, and you said it yourself, he wouldn't tell you where they were from. It's gotta be them."

"No." I shook my head. "He wouldn't do that."

"Well, you don't think it's Ian, do you? Steven said the police stopped by their house last night." She lowered her voice and eyed the crowd in the hallway to make sure no one was listening. "They found out Ian had gone hiking the weekend before the murder. Alone. The perfect chance to bring back a girl and hide her somewhere."

I gasped, though I still didn't believe Ian had done it either. In my mind, the killer was someone evil and nefarious with missing teeth and skull tattoos on their arms. And this person was long gone, probably in Mexico by now. "What did their dad do?"

"What do you think?" she said smugly. "He kicked the police out on their asses."

"Oh." I guess being a hotshot lawyer allowed you to do that sort of thing.

"Come on, Aye." She jiggled my shoulders. "Anyone who knows Ian can tell you he's innocent, but what about Jamie? What do you really know about him? Other than the fact he gives you the down low tingle."

"Stop it." I slammed my door shut and walked away so she couldn't see me blush.

"No, I mean it," she said, chasing after me. "Do you even know his last name?"

I pushed through the hallway, Geometry class in sight, though not really an escape since we were in the same class. "That's not important."

"It totally is. I bet he left it out on purpose so you can't Google it and find out they're wanted in seven states."

I stopped outside the door and faced her. "Just quit, okay. You didn't see the look on his face. He was devastated."

"Devastated that she was killed, or that someone found her?"

I threw up my hands and stomped into the classroom. What was the point of arguing?

"You should listen to me," she said over my shoulder once we'd sat down. "You'll be sorry if you don't."

"Whatever."

I didn't have the energy to deal with fish after school, so I told my dad I had a big test I needed to study for, and he sent me home. It was true about the test. Final exams were coming up after all, but it was also true that Mae's words had made a lot more impact than I'd let on. When I got home and saw Fee in the living room watching her soaps, I ditched my books and joined her instead. History had waited this long for me to discover it. What was a few more hours?

She was lounging on the sofa, her feet on our coffee table made from Dad's old sea chest, her wheelchair a step away. It wasn't that she couldn't walk, but ever since she'd shattered her hip last year, walking had been a lot more difficult. That's why she'd moved in with us. I couldn't have been happier. It gave me someone to hang out with in the afternoons, but more importantly I could talk to her. She wouldn't argue like Mom, or pretend everything was sunshine and roses like Dad.

I curled up against her shoulder, a green and blue afghan spread across both of our laps, and took her hand in mine. Her fingers glinted with two wedding bands: hers on her ring finger, Grandpa Colm's on her thumb. Irish Claddagh rings, in honor of their parents' heritage. She'd told me they were all mine if I ever decided to get married, but I thought they looked better on her.

"What's wrong, little pup?"

I pulled the edge of the afghan up under my chin. "What makes you think something's wrong?"

"You only get this snuggly when you want to talk." She hit the "mute" button on the remote control. "So, tell me. What's got you upset?"

"I'm not upset really." No, that was a lie. As the afternoon dragged on, my thoughts had turned into a tangled mess. Dead girls bound with rope from our store, strange families with stranger habits, small towns where people knew everything and nothing both at the same time. I felt like I was adrift in the chaos. And in the center of it all, was Jamie. "It's . . . a boy."

"Our new neighbors." It wasn't a question, and when I tilted my head up, she gave me a knowing smile.

"You know?"

"My window looks out onto the water too."

"Oh, right." It didn't bother me that she had seen us, because I knew it was an accident. She wouldn't spy. I settled my head back down and picked at a green stripe in the afghan. "Thanks for not telling on me."

"Mmm," she murmured in agreement. "We all need our secrets, don't we?"

"What do you think his secrets are?"

"The Flannigans?" She laughed, a deep, throaty sound full of joy and life. "Whatever you've heard, they're just an old sea family. That house has been in their family for generations. I went to school with his grandparents."

"So you know them?"

"Yes, and I'm not surprised to see them come back." She moved her hand up to my head and pressed it against her shoulder, a welcome hug. "They're good people. I think that boy is a wonderful match for you."

I didn't know about matches. I was only sixteen after all. But the rest made me feel a lot better. Mae's argument became ridiculous once again, and I wondered how I let time and my own mind make me think differently.

Still, when I was alone in my room with my laptop staring at me, I did it. *Flannigan, Jamie. Flannigan, James. Flannigan family, Cannon Beach, Oregon.* I typed them all into Google.

Nothing.

I stuck my tongue out at the computer screen. Take that, Mae.

For the next few days, I buried myself in my painting, a way to pass the time while waiting to hear from Jamie. At first I was antsy. I wanted him to call or stop by. That's what guys did when they liked you, right? Since Ian, I'd been on a couple of group dates, if you could call them that. But since touching fingers over a tub of movie popcorn provided no real frame of reference for a relationship, I was left to wonder about Jamie. What had happened that night? I gave all of my paintings a gray background, the color of an approaching storm.

As more days passed, I grew frustrated and even angry. He'd acted like he liked me and then ran away. What kind of guy does that?

Maybe Fee was wrong. Maybe he wasn't such a great guy. I mean, she didn't know him personally, did she? My paintings turned the color of an angry sunset, fiery oranges and harsh reds.

Eventually, even that faded away and turned into concern. What if something had happened to him? I tried to remember the exact look on his face when I told him about the girl. Was he just upset? Or had he been scared too? Purples and blues.

By Friday night, paint no longer soothed my feelings. I convinced myself something was wrong and I decided to go over to their house first thing in the morning. Even though I knew perfectly well my courage would fade with the night.

Then, at one a.m. according to my cell phone, I was woken by a rhythmic tapping on my window. I rubbed my eyes in case it was a dream, but I opened them again and Jamie was still there. I jumped out of bed and threw open the window, breathing in his light musky scent mixed with ocean brine. The most welcome scent in the world.

"I'm sorry I ran off the other night," he whispered before I had the chance to say anything.

I wanted to tell him it was fine, but once I saw he was okay, I went back to being angry. So I said nothing.

"The girl was my cousin, Deirdre. She disappeared almost a month ago from her home near here. Left a note one night saying she'd gone for a walk. She never came back." He tilted his head just a little and the moonlight highlighted his face. In that moment he looked so old, and so very young. My angry muscles released, and I found it hard to stand without them.

"Oh." I flopped down on my window seat, leaving room for him to climb in and sit beside me. His legs dangled outside while his heels tapped against the gray wooden exterior. "I'm sorry."

He lifted one shoulder and dropped it. "We thought she had run away. She was always threatening to. She didn't get along with her parents, and she was eighteen. She had every right to go. We never dreamed this could have happened to her. The coroner said she died from head injuries. Someone beat her to death and then tossed her . .

." He waved his hand toward the bay, letting the movement finish the sentence for him.

"Oh." So there it was. Deirdre was from here, which meant someone in my sleepy little town was actually a murderer. Maybe my mom was right. Maybe I should curl up in bed and wait for it all to go away. I thought of Fee's crime dramas where the killer was always the super-sweet post office guy, or the quiet bagger at the grocery store. "Do the police have any leads?"

He gazed out to the water, like he was seeking absolution. I wanted to help him find it. "They said maybe, but they didn't seem too sure. My dad doesn't trust them."

"Oh." From the way Ian's dad had reacted to Hansel and Rowe, it seemed Jamie's father wasn't alone in his distrust. "Well, they know who she is now. Maybe that will help them solve this."

"I don't know. Maybe."

My heart broke at the sad sigh in his words. I grasped for something comforting to say, but everything seemed flat compared to losing a family member. I didn't remember Grandpa Colm too well, but I knew the effect it had on those who did. Hoping I didn't sound too lame, I said, "Is there anything I can do?"

He slid his hand across the seat and placed it across the back of mine. His heart beat through his fingertips, pulsing in time to the lapping waves outside.

"My family is having a bonfire tomorrow night, to celebrate her life and to say goodbye. Her parents will be there. Some cousins." He took a slow breath, summoning his next words. "I'd like you to join us."

"You want me to meet your family?" I swallowed, but the nerves hung in my throat like salt in the air.

He lifted his hand and swept the back of it against my cheek, as softly as I imagined his kiss would be. I leaned into the touch. "Please?"

At my nod, he brushed his lips against my forehead. "Thank you."

I watched him take off down the beach, stretching my neck out the window until I lost him in the darkness. My breath staggered under the weight of what had just happened. He kissed me! Okay, it wasn't on the mouth, but it was still amazing.

I wanted to whisper my thanks to the ocean, because I was certain it had brought Jamie and me together, but when my eyes flicked by our pier, they caught on my mom.

She stood facing out to the horizon with her arms clutched around her middle like she was holding something in. She was barefoot, and the hem of her robe wiggled slightly in the breeze. Every now and then, she'd shift her weight from one foot to the other, but apart from that, she didn't move. I wondered what she was thinking. I'd never seen her out there before. Heck, she rarely set foot on the beach, and never without some prodding from Dad or me. Then again, it wasn't like I made a habit of staring out my window at two a.m. Did she do this a lot?

Before I could figure out an answer, she turned around and started walking back toward the house. It may have been a trick of the night, but I swore I saw her wipe a tear away from her cheek.

Maybe she missed Grandpa Colm. He'd been lost to the sea, right? That must have been it. Otherwise, why would she cry?

The next morning, Fee and I got up and fixed breakfast. Scrambled eggs, toast, bacon, and coffee. Yes, it was a cheap ploy, but sometimes you do what you have to. Dad wouldn't have a problem with me going out, but Mom? If she ever got "No!" tattooed across her forehead in sparkly pink letters, I wouldn't be surprised. Hence, the united front.

By the time my parents dragged themselves into the kitchen, we'd stuffed some sea grass in a vase, and set the table with matching silverware and four un-chipped plates. Centered in the table were three steaming pans on hot pad holders, ready and waiting for all to enjoy. I stood with my shoulders squared behind Fee's wheelchair, and the two of us smiled like angels.

Dad brightened his eyes and started singing a song from some 1950s musical about mornings and waking up, while Mom rolled her eyes and poured herself a cup of coffee. She drank half of it while she stood at the counter, then she topped it off. I wondered if her excessive need for caffeine was brought on by frequent nighttime excursions, or if last night had been an isolated event. If anyone else knew about it, they didn't show it, and I wasn't about to ask. Not today.

Mom narrowed her eyes in suspicion. "What are you two planning?"

"Whatever it is," Dad said as he heaped eggs on his plate, "I'm glad they included me."

"Sit down." I pulled out Mom's chair. "Enjoy the meal. And you can brag to everyone at the store today about how wonderful your daughter is."

"Uh huh," she said like she didn't believe it at all. But at least she did it with a wink so I knew not to abandon hope. Now for the next part of the plan.

Fee waited until everyone was eating, and Mom had a mouth full of food, before she spoke. "It appears your daughter has found herself a suitor in the neighbor boy."

Mom froze mid-chew. I giggled because . . . suitor? Dad sat up straight looking slightly impressed.

"Go on," Mom muffled around her toast.

"And she's been invited to attend an event this evening."

Mom shook her head. "Absolutely not. She's grounded."

"My two weeks were up yesterday," I said. "Besides, I'll just be out back . . . on the beach."

"The beach?" Mom raised an eyebrow.

"Not the water," I clarified. "And his whole family will be there. Plenty of parental supervision." I dangled the words in front of her. Her words. The ones that were supposed to unlock my chains.

Mom pinched her face tight. "I don't think so. We don't know those people."

"Fee does," I said.

When Mom looked at her, she nodded. I could have sworn something else passed between them, a question or a bit of knowledge. "She's a good girl, Ciara. Let her go."

Mom turned to Dad. "What do you think about this?"

Dad broke into a grin. I could just make out his dimples beneath his beard. "I think she's been working hard for the past few weeks and deserves to have a little fun."

"What if I went with you to meet his family?" Mom asked.

"No!" Fee and I both shouted. Why couldn't she just say yes for once instead of making this a huge ordeal? It was practically our freaking back yard.

"Please, Mom. You can meet him when he picks me up."

Mom set down her fork very slowly and with great purpose. A jumble of thoughts flashed through her eyes as she did so. She made one last pleading glance to Fee, who responded with a firm nod. "Fine," she said. "But be home by midnight."

"Yes!" I jumped out of my chair, arms wide, and hugged my mom. And for a brief second, she even smiled.

# Chapter Five

"I'll sing you a song, a good song of the sea, with a way, hey, blow the man down . . ." I sang loudly in my dad's shop while shelving buckets of bait in the glass door refrigerator. I'd been so excited about the bonfire, I'd volunteered to work today. Though I think it had more to do with occupying myself instead of pacing my bedroom floor until seven tonight when Jamie was supposed to pick me up. ". . . And hope that you'll join in the chorus with me."

Mont's voice piped in over my shoulder. "Give me some time to blow the man down."

I turned around, laughing.

"You're in a good mood today," he said as he handed me the last two buckets.

"That's because my little girl has a date tonight." Dad squeezed my arm as he passed by on his way to the storeroom.

"Hang on." Mont's tanned, crinkly face lifted into a teasing smile. "Ain't you still ten?"

"And a little bit over," I said, blushing.

"Well, I'll be. Where is your fellow taking you tonight? A fancy dinner? Dancing?" He grabbed one of my hands, put his other on my waist, and started twirling me in circles.

I giggled, trying not to fall. "Nothing like that. The girl in the bay was his cousin. His family is having a memorial bonfire on the beach tonight."

"Tonight?" He stopped, suddenly letting go of me.

I stumbled against the register counter, and when I straightened up, I saw his smile had gone.

"Mont?" His eyes glazed over in a faraway look. I snapped my fingers in front of his nose. No response. "What's wrong? Should I call my dad?"

He grabbed my hand and held it like a vice between the two of us. It *hurt*. "Tonight's the full moon," he said in a rough whisper. "The sea opens up on nights like these."

"Um, okay," I said, wrenching my hand from his and shaking the feeling back down to my fingers. Mont's sudden departures from reality weren't uncommon. Standard procedure was to humor him until they passed. Dad said it was a result of too many days at sea. The sun and isolation did things to sailors. "And what should I expect?"

His eyes widened. He balled his hands up beside his cheeks and popped them open. "Magic." Then, he laughed and walked away. Moments later, he'd grabbed a broom and was whistling and sweeping like the conversation had never happened.

I'd changed outfits three times. What were you supposed to wear to a bonfire that's also a wake? A dress? Pants and a blouse? Jeans and a t-shirt? I decided on the latter since that's what I was most comfortable in, though I would keep watch out my window, and if Jamie passed by in something dressier, I would change.

Fortunately, he'd gone with beach casual just like me, and at 7:00 on the dot, he was knocking on our back door.

Mom, for the most part, was on her best behavior. Dad was welcoming, and Fee treated him like family. I only wanted to sink into the floor once, and that was when Mom pulled Jamie aside. I don't know what she said, but he came away red-faced and at a loss for words. Once we were out the door, I asked what she'd done. He just shook his head and said, "She wants you to be safe. That's all."

Most of Jamie's family was already at the fire. And by family, I meant parents, aunts, uncles, cousins, grandparents—the whole deal. There must have been forty or fifty people there. They'd set up the fire in an alcove of rocks maybe halfway between our two houses and a good distance away from the water. People sat on the rocks, leaned against them, roasted hot dogs around the fire, and talked.

Jamie led me to a small group sitting at the back of the alcove. "Aileen, this is my mom Caitlin, my dad Liam, and my sister Bridget," he said, pointing to each of them in turn. They all had the same dark hair, though his dad's hair was short and curly. His mom and sister each had straight, waist-length hair, and Bridget was the only one who didn't share the family's brown eyes. Hers were a deep sea blue. She was busy texting someone, but waved and smiled when she was introduced. His parents each shook my hand.

"I'm sorry to hear about your niece," I said.

"Thank you," Mr. Flannigan said. "I'm so glad you could help us celebrate her life. Family is very important to us."

Jamie's mom nodded her agreement, and the warmth, not only in their faces, but in their bodies too, made me feel instantly welcome.

"So Jamie tells us you're quite an artist," his mom said with a smile.

I shrugged, not wanting to brag, but happy that Jamie had talked about me. "I paint what I like, what speaks to me."

"Which is?" Bridget asked.

"This." I swept my arm in an arc, indicating the living, breathing world that was my own backyard.

"It's inspiring, isn't it?" his dad asked. "I don't know how anyone could stand living away from the sea."

"Neither do I."

The sun hovered just over the horizon, stalling, as if she didn't quite trust the moon to take over for the night. My fingers itched for a paintbrush like they always did this time of day. The colors and sounds and smells made me feel like I was standing on the edge. Of what, I couldn't say exactly, but my toes dug into the sand, wanting to jump.

Jamie's fingers closed around mine, bringing me out of my reverie. I turned back to his family. Bridget was focused once again on her phone, but his parents were looking at me like they completely understood me. Like I belonged.

"Come on," Jamie said. "Let's get something to eat."

On our way to the food table, Jamie threw his arm around my shoulders. "They're crazy about you."

I laughed. "They just met me."

"Oh," he said with a twinkle in his eyes. "Maybe that's me then."

I'd never seen a more perfect sunset, though I was pretty sure it had more to do with my company than nature's beauty. Jamie and I sat together on the edge of the alcove, leaning against one of the rocks, his arm draped around me. When I got up the courage, I tilted my head to his shoulder. He must have welcomed it, because I heard a low sigh escape his lips. That sound and the warmth of his breath brushing against the top of my head, sent shivers down my spine.

Once the sun finally gave up the sky, everyone settled quietly around the fire, right alongside a bit of unexpected company. A young harbor seal caterpillar crawled up the beach and came to a rest beside me. She was light gray with black spots and a dark charcoal smear under her left eye. I placed my hand on her back and she exhaled, spreading her flippers out at her sides and stretching her face toward the crackling fire.

Jamie's face twisted into an amused grin. "Friend of yours?"

"Leilani," I said, feeling the coarse fur beneath my fingers. "She was born on the rocks behind my house last summer."

"Do you have any paintings of her?"

I shook my head. "Not since she was barely a day old."

Leilani twisted her head in my direction as if to say, "Well get on with it, will you?"

I laughed. "Next week, okay?"

And she settled back down.

Jamie squeezed my shoulder, drawing my attention back to him and his strange, cockeyed smile.

"What?" I asked suspiciously.

"Most people have dogs or cats for pets."

I scrunched my shoulders and tried to hide the heat creeping into my cheeks. "I know, I'm weird."

"Not so weird. Take a look." He pointed toward the water where a few other seals were emerging from the waves, heading not to me, but to various other spots around the fire.

Jamie's family welcomed the seals in a way my own family never would have, meaning, they smiled and waited for the animals to situate themselves, while my mom would've chased them away with a broom. "Disease," she'd claim. "Can't be too careful." It was all I could do to convince her I needed to get close enough to snap photos for my paintings. She would have grasped her chest and had a coronary out of spite if she knew I ever interacted with them. It was a relief to be around people who accepted that side of me, and even shared my little quirks.

Once everyone had arrived, Deirdre's mother stood up and welcomed everyone. She didn't have many words. Who would in her situation? Instead she invited others to share theirs. She only had one rule: make people smile.

For the next hour or so, people stepped up and told stories about Deirdre. About her love of thrift store shopping and her unique style no one understood but her. About how she craved the night time, often coming home with a huge smile on her face and sealed lips. About every silly, funny memory there was, including her obsession with clear gummy bears, which were passed around in a large bowl for all to enjoy.

Towards the end, Jamie got up. He stood in the same place everyone else did, in the very center between Deirdre's parents. He tugged the bottom of his t-shirt, another tour one from some band I'd never heard of, cleared his throat, then focused into the fire. His voice was low, but steady. "A few months ago, Deirdre came to see me. She said she was leaving and wanted to say goodbye. We took a walk along the beach, and I tried to talk her out of it. She smiled and told me not to worry, that no one would miss her. But right about then, she looked down and spotted some sea glass." He glanced down at her mom. "She remembered what you always said, that they were mermaid tears shed over the loss of a loved one."

She nodded, and a few others smiled or murmured their agreement.

Jamie focused back on the fire, its flames lifting the story into the night, and maybe to Deirdre's ears. "I think that piece of glass reminded her that someone would miss her, because she went home and started collecting more pieces. She'd go out almost every day at low tide, searching for them. She knew your twenty-fifth wedding anniversary was coming up, and she wanted to find twenty-five pieces and make a necklace for you. The last time I spoke to her—" Jamie's voice broke. I swallowed as if I were the one speaking. He took a deep breath and pressed on. "The last time I spoke to her, she'd only found twenty-two pieces. I knew where she kept the necklace, so I took it." He reached into his pocket and pulled it out, his hand balled around something. "I spent three days searching for those last pieces. And, um," his voice broke again, "here." He opened his hand and a necklace with green and blue and clear glass dangled from his fingers. Simple and perfect. He dropped it into her mom's hand. She accepted it wordlessly, and Jamie headed back to his seat.

As Jamie passed by, Deirdre's dad touched his hand. He looked up at Jamie, and the fire shone on his face. "Thank you," he said. Then a single tear rolled down her father's cheek. The only one that night.

After the stories were over, the crowd broke up into smaller groups, but no one went home. A bunch of the younger kids ran down to the water's edge to splash in the bright moonlight. The seals returned to the ocean, floating out there like soda bottles, the top halves of their bodies bobbing above the water. Jamie's parents headed off on a walk along with a few others, and Bridget scooted up to us, her phone still clutched in her hand.

"Hey, little brother," she said with a slightly crooked smile that reminded me a lot of his.

"No," he answered immediately. "Not tonight."

Her phone beeped with a text and when she glanced at it, the light from the fire caught the determined glow in her eyes. "Please."

"This is the third time in a week. I'm tired of covering for you and Kyle. Just tell Mom and Dad what you're doing."

"They'll kill me," she whined. "Besides," she looked pointedly at me, "someday you're gonna want my help and I'd hate to deny you."

Jamie shook his head. "I don't have to sneak out. Mom and Dad have no problems with Aileen."

A small part of me filled with pride. Jamie's parents liked me.

Bridget's phone beeped again, and her tone grew more desperate. "You don't have to lie. Just tell them Ashlyn came to pick me up, and I'm spending the night at her house."

Jamie raised one of his eyebrows. "Is that really what you're doing?"

"As far as you know? Yes." Then she typed in a frantic reply on her phone and jumped to her feet. As she took off down the beach, she turned around and blew her brother a kiss. "I owe you one!"

Jamie settled back against the rock and sighed. "Whatever."

"Let me guess," I said. "She's not going to spend the night with Ashlyn."

"Nope. It's some guy she met a couple of weeks ago. Mom and Dad really would kill her if they found out."

"Then why do you help her?"

"Because she's my sister, and if I didn't, she'd find some other way to make my life miserable. Besides," he tucked me in the crook of his arm, "there are other things I'd rather focus on tonight."

I had to admit, I liked the change of subject. "Such as?"

A log shifted on the fire, and a shower of sparks shot up into the night. "That," he said, and I knew exactly what he meant.

There were a few people still around, but I didn't notice them. All I could think about was Jamie and what this night held for us. We sat together in the alcove, his arm around me, our heads turned to each other. Enough distance between us to appear innocent, but close enough to feel maddening.

"Thank you for coming," he said. "I know you didn't know Deirdre but—"

"No," I said. The more I'd heard about her, the more I wished I'd known her. And the more I felt like I did. "I'm glad you invited me. It was beautiful."

He brushed his thumb against my cheek. "So are you."

I think my heart stopped. No one but my dad had ever said that to me, and the difference was breathtaking. Jamie dropped his hand to his lap, but I could still feel the hot trail his thumb had left across my face. I studied his lips, the little pinching movements they made, the way his tongue slid across them, and I wondered if he wanted to kiss me. And would he? Of the few people around, no one was paying attention to us.

"She's seventeen, Caitlin," Mr. Flannigan's voice whisper/shouted through the air. "She has no idea what she's doing!"

Jamie and I peeked up over the rock we'd been leaning against. His parents stood behind us in the shadows about twenty feet away. We'd been too preoccupied to notice they'd come back from their walk.

"You know she's only acting out because you're pushing her. You need to ease up. I refuse to let her end up like Deirdre."

"Then you talk to her, because right now I am beyond furious!" Mr. Flannigan cast his eyes around the area. Orange flashes of firelight danced across his face, making him seem even angrier than he sounded. I slid down so he couldn't see me behind the rock. If he asked me where Bridget had gone, I would have a hard time lying.

Maybe Jamie read my mind because the next words out of his mouth were, "Do you want to go for a walk?"

We set off in the direction of his house.

"Sorry about that," Jamie said once we were out of hearing distance.

"It's okay." I shrugged it off. "You stick around me long enough, I'm sure you'll see my mom lose it once or twice."

"I'd like that." He gave me a wide grin, then his eyes went round as saucers as he realized what he'd just said. "I mean the sticking around part. Not the . . ." He held his hand up like a puppet and mimed it yelling at some invisible person.

I smiled, and with that little bit of encouragement, his face twisted into an exaggerated frown. His mouth opened and closed in a silent tirade as his fingers chomped the air.

I broke into giggles, so his impersonation grew even goofier. His other hand joined in, and there were sound effects, cannonballs, and I think some exploding dynamite. Still laughing, I grabbed one of his hands to stop him before he lost a finger. "Enough. I get it."

His body stilled, and his expression grew serious. With an adorable quirk at the corner of his mouth, he said, "I know you do."

We continued on our walk, holding hands and saying little. We couldn't take our eyes off each other, and once we were sufficiently out of sight, he grabbed me by the waist and pulled me to him. It was a shock, feeling his body pressed against mine, but one I had been longing for. I lifted my hands to his shoulders and pressed my fingers into his muscles, urging him closer. His chest rose and fell against mine. He leaned down and I half closed my eyes, needing . . . wanting . . .

". . . have to catch me first!"

"Challenge accepted!"

We both pulled back at the sound of Jamie's cousins rushing past us, though we didn't let go of each other.

Jamie cocked his eyes to the left. "There's a cave . . . a little further down . . ."

I knew exactly the spot he was talking about. It was a wall of rocks, maybe a block or so past Jamie's house, stretching from the grass to the water's edge. The cave sat right around the halfway point, safe from even high tides. The perfect spot for a little . . . um . . . friendly bonding. I smiled. "Let's go."

We half ran/half stumbled in our eagerness to get there. But just as we were passing Jamie's house, we heard a soft cry coming from the tall grass to our left. We stopped to see what it was.

A moment later, I screamed.

# Chapter Six

Bridget lay sprawled in the grass, a diagonal slit running from her ribs to below her belly button. I couldn't tell how shallow or deep it was. All I could see was the blood.

Jamie dropped to his knees, felt the pulse on her neck, and nearly crumpled in relief. Her rattly intake of breath confirmed what he said—she was still alive. Her hands and knees were covered in sand, like she'd crawled there, though I couldn't tell from where.

As Jamie ripped off his shirt to tie around her waist, she whispered one word. "Daddy."

"Get my parents," Jamie shouted.

And I did, before my nausea took over.

As I ran, the sand wrapped around my toes and made me stumble. Questions pelted my mind like hail in a thick, hard rain. Who would do such a thing? Slice open her stomach, then leave her for dead. She was seventeen, for God's sake. And Deirdre hadn't been much older.

The bonfire came into view. Jamie's mom saw me first and rushed to meet me. I spit out what I'd seen and fumbled in my pocket for my cell phone, feeling stupid for not having thought of it before. "I'll call 9-1-1."

Jamie's uncle put his hand on mine. "We'll take care of it."

"Where's her dad? She wanted her dad."

"Don't worry about it," he said as his footsteps carried him down the beach toward Bridget. "I'll find him."

After that, the beach fell into chaos, with people rushing off in a dozen different directions. Some took off with Jamie's mom and uncle. Some ran to claim their children from the water and take them home. A few waited near the alcove, pacing and biting their nails. No one talked to me though, so I sank down against one of the rocks, wrapped my arms around my legs, and dropped my chin to my knees. It occurred to me that I should go home. This was a family thing, and I was in the way. But I couldn't leave until I knew Bridget was going to be all right. I looked in the direction of the road. My fingers tapped a frantic drumbeat against my legs. Where was that ambulance?

After a long, long time that was probably only a few minutes, Jamie's family came back. His uncle cradled Bridget in his arms. She had a couple of different t-shirts, ripped into strips and wrapped around her stomach. She'd bled through all of them. Her skin was pale as paper. Her head flopped back, her long hair nearly dragging the ground.

I sprang to my feet, and Jamie ran to meet me.

"Is she . . ." I tore my eyes away from her limp and lifeless body. "Is she okay?"

He glanced at his uncle, who was carrying Bridget up the steps of their back porch. "We think so," he said, but doubt clung firmly to his words.

"Is there anything I can do?"

He refocused on me, studied me for a moment. Then he pulled me into his arms, tighter than anyone had ever held me before. I squeezed back, knowing as his breath shuddered and his heart pounded against me, that this was what he needed me to do. And I was glad to do it. In fact, I had trouble standing myself, as if the storm that had begun in him had engulfed me as well. All the horror and fear of the night rained down on me, drenching, drowning, soaking me to the bone.

The two of us clung to each other for what seemed like an eon, but eventually, the storm passed and we found ourselves on dry land. With one last sniff, he slid his hands down to mine, and said, "I should get you home."

Sunday passed with me obsessively flipping through the TV and refreshing Google news on my laptop. It kept me busy and numb, so I didn't have to picture Bridget lying in a pool of her own blood. I hadn't told my parents about the attack; Jamie had asked me not to. He'd figured out from his private chat with my mom that she'd dig a dungeon and lock me in it if she knew anything. Not an ideal place to spend a second date. But I also knew it was a matter of time before she heard. Hence my stalking of the news. Deirdre's face was still plastered all over the place, so Bridget should be appearing soon. If I heard the official story, I could come up with something to tell my mom that would remove me from the situation.

By late evening when I'd still found nothing, I started to wonder. Were the police keeping it quiet? Did they know who did it and were waiting until they got the guy before they said anything? That's where my hopes were, because honestly, I refused to think of the alternative, that they were still as clueless I was.

By Monday morning, I was bursting with anxiety. I told Mae I had to talk to her and to meet me at lunch by the firs, our favorite place to gossip. Since the trees were on the edge of school property far away from the cafeteria, and most of the girls had no desire to sit in the dirt while eating lunch, it was the perfect place to talk. People didn't even go there to make out. They did that over in the P.E. shed. Of course, when I saw her approaching with Steven and Ian in tow, I thought she'd gotten the wrong idea. Ever since she'd convinced herself that Jamie was evil, she'd been on a mission to hook me up with Ian. She was now dating his brother, and after spending one afternoon with the two of them, she had decided Ian was my soul mate.

"He's changed," she kept telling me. "I promise."

As she plopped down beside me, I gave her the stink eye she deserved.

"What?" Mae asked innocently. I could practically see her polishing her halo.

"You know what." I nodded toward the boys, who'd settled themselves beside us. Ian stared past me, frowning, while Steven picked at the grass, doing his best to not be involved.

"Sorry, but as your BFF, it's my duty to save you from potential harm. After today, I don't think you'll be taking moonlit strolls with Jamie Flannigan anymore."

"Geez, do you have to blab everything?" I'd sworn her to secrecy when I told her that. I should have known better. The boys at least had the decency not to comment, although Ian's frown deepened.

"This is for your own good, Aye. They're here because they have something to tell you about what happened Saturday night, on the beach by your house," she added with a hint of conspiracy.

"What?" My attention snapped to the boys. From what I had seen, no one knew about the attack on Bridget. "What did you hear?"

The two of them exchanged a look. Stephen spoke up. "After the police left our house last night, I overheard—"

"Wait!" Mae squeaked. "The police came to see you again? Why?"

Ian gave Steven a sharp look, but Steven answered her question. "Well, it turns out Ian knew that girl we found in the bay."

"I don't think 'knew' is the right word," Ian grumbled. "She was just some girl I met at a party. We hung out one night. I hadn't seen her since."

"But you didn't admit it when we were first questioned."

"No one would have recognized her the way we found her!"

"No," Steven agreed. "But the point is, once she was identified and they obtained an actual picture of her, some other kid told on him."

"Wow. So, did you and that girl . . ." Mae let her wiggling eyebrows do the asking for her.

Ian looked at me, but I couldn't tell if he did or didn't want me to know this next part. "Well, maybe a little . . ."

I held up my hand. "No details. I don't want to hear about your stupid conquests." Mae needed to check her definition of "change." He may not have been hooking up with girls from our school anymore, but that didn't mean he'd stopped.

Ian blew out a breath and said, "Look. That was months ago. I didn't do anything to that girl, okay?"

"I know you didn't," Steven assured him. "*We* know you didn't." He looked at both Mae and me. She nodded solemnly in agreement. I shrugged, wishing Ian had stayed in the cafeteria. Trying to be friends with him for Mae's sake was not going to work.

"Our dad knows it too," Steven continued. "That's why he locked himself in his study after the police left. We just happened to overhear a very interesting phone conversation."

"About?" I said, eager to get away from the subject of Ian's extracurricular activities.

"Your boyfriend's family." Mae smiled, proud she knew that part.

"And the way their girls keep getting attacked," Steven added. "Mae said you were there Saturday night. Is it true? Did you see anything?"

They all looked to me to confirm this bit of information. I nodded slowly. "What else?"

Steven continued. "He said the girl we found in the bay was also part of Jamie's family, but when they came to collect the body, they wouldn't give any info about her. They wouldn't say how long she'd been missing or give the names of any of her friends. Dad also said this time Jamie's family will make sure it stays quiet. There won't be any police poking around. Not anywhere."

"Looks like we know who's responsible for the attacks," Ian said to me. "The next time Hansel and Rowe come banging on my door, I know where I'm going to send them."

I couldn't believe what I was hearing. "So you're saying Jamie's relatives are attacking their own kids?"

"Well, they are a little weird!"

"Oh, really?" He was willing to pin this on anyone else, including my boyfriend, when the strongest evidence pointed to him. "If you're so innocent, then where were you Saturday night?"

Ian squared his shoulders. "I was at home, alone. Not that it's any of your business."

Like I believed that. "No random date? Isn't that a little unusual for you?"

"How would you know?"

"Are you really asking me that? Remember eighth grade? The winter formal?"

"I remember not regretting my choice!"

"Guys, stop it," Mae jumped in.

I closed my mouth. I didn't have the words to respond anyway. I may have been crazy about Jamie, but Ian was my first crush. It hurt that I had meant so little to him. And it hurt even more that he didn't look the slightest bit sorry for what he said.

When it was clear the shouting match was over, Mae turned to Steven. "So, did your dad say anything else?"

"Um, yeah, he did."

"And?"

He lowered his voice, as if he wasn't sure he should repeat any more. "He said he was glad the police weren't involved Saturday night, because it would make things easier for him."

"To do what?"

"That's the question," Ian said. And then just for me, he added, "I'll bet the Flannigans have an answer."

What Ian had suggested was impossible. He hadn't heard the stories about Deirdre, hadn't seen Jamie's breakdown. Jamie's entire family had been devastated, and I was certain they knew no more than I did.

But if that was true, why would Jamie's family keep it quiet? We had what amounted to a serial killer loose in our tiny, little town. Shouldn't people be alerted? Mom said that after Deirdre, a town curfew had been a hot topic at the Pack 'n Save. It's not like I wanted to be in lock down, but I had to admit I was freaking out. How close had the killer been to me? Had he been attacking Bridget when Jamie was trying to kiss me? Why hadn't anyone heard her scream? Had he run off when he heard us coming?

And why would the police's lack of involvement make things easier for Ian and Steven's dad? Ian may have been an asshole, but he wasn't a murderer. His dad, on the other hand, exuded enough power for even the police to back away from him. Was it possible he was the attacker? He had known about Saturday night after all. And as for the attack on Deirdre, Ian had bought the rope for his dad, and it was still unaccounted for. She had been found tangled in the propeller of *Mr. Glenn's* boat. The police blamed Ian because he'd been there that night, but what if Deirdre had been caught under there longer than anyone knew? My heart nearly stopped at the thought of her floating there, her dead eyes watching me as I climbed on board that night.

Of course, even if Mr. Glenn *was* guilty, no one in this town would dare accuse him. When a gang of kids had spray painted the front windows of the Pack 'n Save last year, he was the one who prosecuted them and made sure they not only cleaned the store, but helped build a new playground in the park. He was also the one who insisted his sons pay for their crime of stealing the boat. It didn't make sense, unless his dedication to the law was really just a cover for his own crimes.

My mind was still reeling, imagining Mr. Glenn as our very own Jekyll and Hyde, bubbly potions and all, when I followed my parents into the elementary school auditorium for our monthly town meeting. Due to tonight's topic, nearly a thousand people had packed themselves into the auditorium, which meant that over two hundred were left standing, crowding the aisles and demanding answers. I hadn't seen this large of a turn out since last year when Mrs.

Sandowski won a contest, bringing some star from General Hospital to our town to speak. Fee had dragged me to that one, and the guy was pretty hot, so who was I to complain? This time, it wasn't such a drool worthy occasion. People, myself included, wanted to know about the murdered girl. Unfortunately, I doubted our police officers had a clue.

Rowe took the podium, standing in the center of the stage with cardboard cut-outs of Little Red Riding Hood's forest as his backdrop. He tapped the microphone, sending a squeal of feedback through the hall. Most people covered their ears, letting the few outspoken voices complain for them.

"Uh, sorry," Rowe grunted. "I'm here tonight because Mayor Talbot asked me to speak to you."

"It's about time," called a man from the back.

"Have you caught anyone yet?" someone else shouted.

Rowe's eyebrow bunched up in concentration. "We are investigating some leads."

Well, that was nice and vague. I craned my neck to see Mr. Glenn, who was sitting in the same row, but on the opposite side of the auditorium from me. He sat straight, shoulders squared, and wore an impressive poker face. Before I'd always thought he carried a no-nonsense air about him. Now he seemed sort of creepy.

My mom shouted out to Rowe, "In other words, you have no clue. What's being done to protect our kids?"

"Yeah!" came a voice to the far right.

Rowe cleared his throat. "We have every reason to believe this was an isolated incident, and no further safety measures are required."

Again, I watched Mr. Glenn. While his sons squirmed beside him, he sat perfectly still, taking in every word Rowe was saying. Allowing him to give our town false information when he knew the truth and, unlike me, he had answers.

And since he did have answers, wasn't it his job to help the police? If he was hiding things, that meant he was working against them.

That fact alone made me more convinced than ever he had something to do with the attacks.

If I had the guts to speak up, if I hadn't promised Jamie I'd keep quiet, would Mr. Glenn confess what he knew, or would he come up with some lie to make me look like an idiot? There was no one else in the auditorium who had seen Bridget, her family included, so it would be my word against his. Oh God, I really wished I didn't know about Bridget, because then I wouldn't be thinking that I could be sitting in the same room as a murderer.

"As always," Rowe continued, "we urge you to be smart. Know where your kids are at all times. Set a curfew. Don't let them go out at night alone and make sure they have a means to reach you in case of trouble."

Mr. Glenn shouted, "Hear, hear!" and a few others joined in, not wanting to argue with the most powerful man in town. I felt like I was gonna be sick.

Mom humphed and slumped back in her seat. Dad put his hand on hers. Somehow I didn't think, "Give your kid a cell phone," was what she wanted to hear. And as much as I hated to admit it, I had to agree.

"What about vagrants?" came a woman's voice from the back. "I've seen lights in some of those abandoned fishing cabins and fires on the beaches at night. Murderers. Transients. Our town is going to ruin and all you can give us are vague answers."

Rowe cleared his throat, as if he'd been caught off guard. "If you'd like to fill out a report—"

"You're asking me to do paperwork?"

"Well, no. It's simply—"

"Madam," a strong, deep voice bellowed from the front row, "I believe I can help with your issue." He strode toward the stage with a cardboard tube in his hand, climbed the steps, and took up a place beside Rowe as if he'd been invited up there.

The shark.

Rowe gave the man a once-over, like he didn't want to relinquish the podium, but he must have sensed he was sinking and burning in front of the crowd, so he stepped aside to let someone else try.

"My name is Ben Harwood," the shark said with a broad, toothy smile. "I'm sure some of you recognize me."

A few murmurs went up through the room.

My mom rolled her eyes.

"We had some good times in high school, didn't we?" Ben continued. "Remember when I convinced Principal Blakely to send all of the science classes on that field trip to The Oaks to study amusement park physics?" A few more murmurs, and some smiles. "Or when I organized our senior class project, and we received special recognition from the governor for building Seal Bay Park?"

"I still have the photos," called a man from the left side of the room.

Ben pointed at him and winked. "I'd like to see those, Mark. Why don't you come by sometime?"

"Will do."

Ben smiled and continued. "What about homecoming 1988, when I single handedly retrieved our mascot from the Providence Pirates? Never mind that our goat came back with a bathing suit and curly, yellow wig." That got some laughter, and Ben surveyed the crowd, beaming. He had them now. "Anyway, I think what I'm trying to say is, you trust me, don't you? I get things done. And I have a plan to whip this town back into shape." He pulled a poster from the tube and unrolled it, revealing a colorful drawing with "Seal Bay Traders" marked across the top. I cringed at the sight of our store replaced with a pink and green monstrosity. "When's the last time you went down to Main Street?"

People shouted out their answers.

"A couple of weeks ago."

"Last month."

"I go to the Super Walmart in Coos Bay."

Ben pointed a finger at that last comment. "Bingo. And why do you avoid Main Street?" Before the man could say anything, Ben supplied the answer. "Because it's filthy, run down, and smelly."

Did he just insult our shop? Seriously, we sold live bait. Smell was part of the deal. I looked to my dad, hoping he would say something, but he kept a stony face. How could he listen to this garbage?

"Here's the solution." Ben held the drawing up over his head like a banner. "Clean up Main Street, we clean up our town. We present an image that criminals aren't welcome here; that we respect our community too much to allow anything like this to happen again."

A cheer went through the crowd. I sunk down into my seat. He'd promised them nothing but a pretty store, and they'd bought into it hook, line, and sinker.

As Ben folded up his drawing and went back to his seat, people began chatting with each other about the exciting changes. Amid the commotion, I saw Mr. Glenn ease out of his chair and gesture for Ian and Steven to follow him. Just before he left, he looked back across the room with a smug smile on his face. I doubted anyone noticed it but me, and even if they had, they would have no idea what that smile meant. Mr. Glenn was glad the shark had diverted attention from the attacks. It bought him more time. To do what, I didn't know. And how was I supposed to find out?

Once everything settled down, Rowe gave a few more encouraging words, emphasizing procedures that were already in place such as nightly patrols and neighborhood watches, then stepped down, declaring the meeting over.

Most of the adults seemed satisfied with that, and soon they were milling around, discussing their summer plans over red punch and cookies, while the kids split off to do their own socializing. I was about to grab Mae and tell her about Mr. Glenn when I saw the shark quickly approaching. At that, I decided to stick around. He slid up beside my mom and slipped an arm around her shoulder.

"Ciara, so good to see you."

"Ben," she said curtly, while ducking out from under his arm. I hadn't heard the story of why they broke up, but seeing the way he tried to envelop her, like she was a possession, I could imagine why.

My dad's fingers tightened around his clear, plastic cup. The liquid sloshed inside. "You're not getting my store, Harwood."

"Relax." Ben held his palms up like he was surrendering. "I only want to catch up. No more business tonight."

"Or tomorrow," I said. "Or the next day."

"Aileen." My dad gave me a look that clearly said shut up, so I did.

"That's all right." Ben laughed and raised his cup to salute me. "That's one tough little bargainer you have there. If she's anything like your wife, you're gonna have your hands tied."

"That's our girl," Dad said as he patted my shoulder. Mom cracked a smile. I stood up a little taller, choosing to accept the compliment.

"Good. That's good to hear." Ben took a gulp of his punch. "So, Aileen, are you a swimmer like your mom?"

My ego deflated as the air whooshed out of me. "What?"

"Ben," my mom said, shaking her head in warning.

"Aw, Ciara, don't be modest." To me, he said, "Back in high school, your mom was quite the champion swimmer. Won all kinds of trophies. I bet if she put her mind to it, she could even out swim a shark."

What I wanted to ask was, *Did she out swim you?* But what actually came out of my mouth was a very weak, "Mom?" How had she not told me this? She could *swim*? She was a *champion*? I was angry she had never let me learn, but now I felt like I'd been betrayed.

"It was a long time ago." She grabbed me by the elbow, dragging me toward the doors. "Come on. You have school tomorrow. See you later, Ben," she called back over her shoulder, and even he flinched at the venom in her voice.

I stopped by Fish Tales the next afternoon to check my inventory. I was so preoccupied with what had happened the night before, I didn't notice that no one appeared to greet me. Dad insisted on having someone by the register any time a customer was in the store, both to provide service and as a theft deterrent. The fact that he didn't come out when the little brass bell by the front door jingled should have set off alarms in my head, but I didn't hear the alarms because my mind was already filled with noise.

I did a brief count of paintings, reshelved a few things that had either gotten moved or grown legs and walked (according to Mont, that was always a possibility) and went to the register to see if I had an envelope of money waiting for me. That's when their conversation broke through the chatter in my brain.

"They sold last night?" My dad's question traveled through the closed office door. "Really?"

"They deposited the check this morning," a stern male voice answered him. "Honestly, Alex, you're not going to get a better offer than this." I heard the rattle of paper as he added, "And this time I think you'll see I'm being more than generous."

I pressed my ear against the office door and tried not to breathe. I didn't have to see inside the room to know Dad was talking to Ben.

"A two percent increase from the last offer?" Dad's voice was so quiet, so uncommitted, it was almost like he was considering the offer.

*Come on, Dad. What are you thinking? We don't need this guy or his money. There's nothing wrong with Main Street. He can build his box store in some other town.*

Ben spoke again. "I think you'll find your choices are waning. My offer is more than you'll get if the bank forecloses, and according to my sources, you are dangerously close—"

"Get out," my dad growled.

*Yes!* I punched the air.

"Well then, I'll leave you to your, uh," Ben cleared his throat, "business. You have one month to consider the contract. After that, I cut my offer in half."

Footsteps approached the door, and I moved to the register counter, burying my nose in a stack of mail I had no interest in reading.

As Ben exited the office, he paused at the cash register and indicated the painting on the wall behind me. It was a 40" x 20" landscape of the rocks behind my house with at least a dozen seals lounging on them, and the largest painting I had ever done. "Interesting work there. Friends of yours?"

I ignored him, flipping through the mail as if fascinated by the fonts and design of each individual bill, and trying not to flinch at the ones stamped "Urgent!" in bright, red ink.

"Here." He pulled a business card from the depths of his jacket and tucked it into the front of my backpack. It stuck out enough that I could read most of the curly lettering. *Ben Harwood. Entrepreneur. Dealer of art and antiquities.* "Call me. We should talk."

I paused long enough to raise one eyebrow.

He took a step backward, a good show of being offended. But that's all it was. A show. "Well, if you change your mind, you have my card." His mouth crooked up in a smirk as he sauntered toward the door.

Geez, that man had nerve, expecting me to side against my dad. *Never gonna happen.*

I watched the shark climb into his Lexus, made sure he drove away, then poked my head into the office where my dad sat at the card table he used as a desk. He stared blankly at the packet of paper in his hands.

"Dad?"

He quickly shoved the packet under a larger stack. "Oh, hey. I didn't realize you were here."

"Yeah." I wanted to step inside and wrap my arms around his shoulders, but the distant look in his eyes kept me rooted in place. "Are you okay?"

He shook his head and blinked a few times until his eyes focused on me. "Yeah, baby. Listen, I've still got some business here to deal with. Why don't you head home, and I'll see you later." He managed a weak smile, and I forced one back, pretending not to notice how his eyes kept drifting to the contract.

"Sure, Dad. I'll see you later."

As I unlocked my bike from the bike rack out front, I looked next door and spotted something new in the Paws by the Sea window. It was a painting I had done for them of a dog running down the beach at sunset. A paper caption bubble had been taped above his head. "Going out of business sale. One month left. Everything must go, including fixtures and shelves."

I whacked my kickstand harder then I should and yelped when I jammed my toe.

"Dammit," I said, hopping up and down on one foot. "What else?"

The answer came when I got home and sulked off to my bedroom, where I found Jamie slumped on my window seat.

# Chapter Seven

His head was down, his hair draped in front of him. The window behind him was open, my yellow curtains swaying softly in the warm spring breeze.

When my door clicked shut, he looked up, and I could see the ghosts in his eyes. I tried to name them: Fear, Exhaustion, but there was one I couldn't quite identify. I called it Shadow.

I dropped my backpack to the floor and sat beside him. As much as I wanted to dwell on my own problems, they seemed insignificant when I remembered what he was dealing with. "How's Bridget?"

"Better." His voice sounded rough, salty. "She's awake."

"Is she at the hospital, or—"

"No, she's at home."

"Already? Doesn't she need surgery or a transfusion?"

Jamie's hands gripped the edge of the seat tight enough that the cords in his neck stood out.

That alone was enough to answer the question, but the way he wouldn't meet my eyes made me remember what I never saw Saturday night, flashing red lights. "Your uncle never called the ambulance, did he?"

"Doctors can't do anything for her." He sounded so hopeless, like her fate had been written by the sea.

But I didn't believe in fate. "Jamie, she needs a doctor. What if her injuries get infected? She could die."

"She won't die!" He pounded his fists into the cushion, and I jumped to my feet. He blinked, and his face softened. "I'm sorry." He grabbed my fingertips. His anger gone as quickly as it had come. "I'm just . . ."

Scared. "I know." I let him pull me back to him. I sat down, doing nothing but watching him breathe. The air thickened with each intake. Tentatively, I rested my hand on his back, fingers first, then my palm, and pressed small circles between his shoulder blades.

"She needs . . ." His muscles tightened beneath my hand.

"What?"

"My family," he whispered.

"Your . . ." I blinked. "Wait. Is this a religious thing? Because I think her injuries would trump something like that."

"No. That's not it."

"Then, I don't understand. What can your family do that a doctor can't?"

His eyes flicked back and forth between mine. The Shadow ghost swirled in them and then clarified a bit. I froze, waiting. *Tell me. Trust me.* He shook his head and his eyes turned opaque again.

"I can't."

"Jamie, please." I moved my hand to his shoulder, strong and broad, curled over from the weight of the Shadow. I squeezed his muscle, urging him to let me in. His lips trembled, as if the words were about to force their way out. Then he turned away. My hand dropped to my lap.

"It's not my place to tell you."

"Whose—"

"We're not safe here," he added, like it wasn't obvious.

"Why haven't you told the police? They can—"

"No!"

The force of his desperation nearly knocked me over, and I couldn't help but remember Steven's words. *Jamie's family will make sure it stays quiet.* No police. No hospital. "So, you *are* keeping this a secret."

"We have to."

"Why? Your sister's life is at stake, and you're refusing to get her help!"

"You don't know what you're talking about!"

"Who are you protecting?" Mr. Glenn may have been my number one suspect, but I couldn't stop Ian's suspicions from playing in my mind. *I wouldn't be surprised if someone in his family was responsible for both attacks.* What if he was right, and Mr. Glenn was involved in some other way I hadn't figured out yet? Carefully, I asked, "Is it someone in your family?"

"I'm protecting *everyone* in my family," he snapped.

"Not Bridget!"

"Especially her! Do you know what would happen if . . ." He sucked his bottom lip into his mouth and bit down until his eyes watered.

"If what?"

He shook his head. "I can't tell you." And with that, the Shadow solidified into a wall. He may have called it protection, but I called it a lie. Maybe this was the only one. Maybe it was the first of many. Whichever it was, Ian's accusations began to seem possible.

I lowered my voice into a whisper. "Not can't. Won't."

Again, he shook his head, like it would change anything. "I'm sorry."

"Me too." I stood up, my back to him, because I couldn't say it to his face. "If you can't be honest with me, then I think you should go. And . . . don't come back."

I listened, waiting for him to protest or give me a solution, but he didn't say anything else. I turned around to find my window seat vacant, the curtains billowing over it. The emptiness hit me like a shock wave. I ran to the window, my lungs aching to call him back.

But he was gone. The only movement was a distant seal ducking beneath the waves.

My door creaked open later that night. I wasn't surprised. I'd been hiding since Jamie left, ignoring the numerous calls for dinner, blubbering under my covers and beating myself up for doing so. If he couldn't be honest with me, then I couldn't date him. End of story.

Except it wasn't.

What if Jamie couldn't tell me because he didn't know? What if his family was keeping secrets from him? What if he was just as much a victim as Deirdre and Bridget? And that smidge of doubt brought the tears back again.

Someone padded across the room, and when the edge of my bed sank down, I snuck one eye out from beneath my comforter. Mom sat there, holding a TV dinner in her hands, minus the Barney tray.

She set the food on my nightstand and gently pried the edge of the comforter from my hands, uncovering the rest of my face. "Wanna talk?"

I pushed myself up against the wall, but retrieved the edge of my comforter. It had a pink satin binding that ran along its edge I used to rub between my knuckles when I was little. "Boys are stupid," I said.

"Oh, baby." She pushed my stringy, damp hair out of my eyes and smiled. "I was hoping it'd be a long time before you figured that out."

I smiled a little too. "You could have warned me."

She looked at me over the top of her glasses. "Would you have listened?"

I thought for a second, then folded my legs up against my chest. I hadn't imagined talking about this stuff with my mom. That's what Fee was for, to talk to without fear of judgment or criticism. But Mom had been the one to bring me my dinner. Maybe she could help. Maybe she wanted to. "Not before today."

"What do you mean?" She took my chin in her hands, her face suddenly hard. "He didn't try anything, did he?"

I twisted out of her grasp, wondering why I opened my mouth. "No, Mom. Nothing like that." I wished it were that simple. At least then I could hate him. But he'd seemed so sad, so lost this afternoon. Had I done the wrong thing?

"Aileen?" Her forehead crinkled just above her nose. Great. Now she was worried.

I spit out the only thing I could think of. "I'm just confused."

"About?"

I smoothed the blanket across my knees. "How do you know you can trust someone?"

"Short answer?" she asked. "You don't."

Typical mom answer. I straightened my legs, tugged on the edge of my comforter, and prepared to disappear again.

"Wait." She pressed her hand against my knees, stopping me. "You didn't hear the long answer."

I stopped, listened. I might have given her an impatient glare.

"You may not ever know if you can trust someone else. But you can always trust yourself. What do your instincts say?"

What did they say? Everything was so muddled. If it was just the way he looked at me, and the feelings I got when he touched me, I might have been able to stay away from him, and hope that was enough. But if I listened to my instincts, I knew that wasn't entirely it. Yes, physically he gave me tingles as Mae had so eloquently pointed out. But there was another feeling that went even deeper. I tried to convince myself I could no longer see that image of us together in twenty years, but it was still there, twisting itself into my soul. It was like when he hooked his finger around mine that one night on the beach. We were tangled together, and I didn't know how to get untangled.

"Okay," I said, because I wanted to be alone again. Maybe I'd Google instincts and how to reverse them. "Thanks."

"You're welcome." Mom squeezed my hand, then plopped my dinner, a silver paper tray full of gelatinous Salisbury steak, into my lap. "Now, eat. I work too hard for you to waste food."

# Chapter Eight

The next afternoon, I had Mom drive me over to Fish Tales so I could drop off some more paintings, and to get the envelope of cash I'd forgotten the day before. After claiming it, I poked my head in the office to thank my dad and tell him I'd gotten the money. He was sitting in the narrow room with a frown on his face, punching his calculator and scribbling furiously in his accounting book. It looked strange on him, the frown, as if he were wearing a mask that didn't fit right.

"Dad?" I came in and shut the door behind me. "About yesterday . . ."

He put down his pen and plastered on a smile. "We'll be fine, pumpkin."

"That's what you always say." I stepped closer so I could read his chicken scratch. I didn't know much about accounting, but I knew negative numbers were bad. Mom's job helped, paid the mortgage, but not much else. There were a lot of months where the only things we ate were pasta or damaged food she brought home from the Pack 'n Save. Dad sometimes needed a little extra kick, especially since Ben's contract sat conspicuously on the corner of the table. Why hadn't he ripped it apart yet?

I eyed the stack of twenty dollar bills in my envelope and sighed. Another delay for my car fund. I set the money beside my dad's book and headed toward the door.

"Aileen," he called.

I looked back over my shoulder. "Yeah, Dad?"

His smile disappeared as his fingers slowly closed over the envelope. "Thank you."

"You're welcome," I said, trying to keep my face casual. It was the first time he hadn't offered to give it back. Not that I would have accepted it, but if things had gotten that bad, why hadn't he said anything? I was too afraid to ask the question. I just hovered there in the doorway until he turned back to his book. Then I bolted.

In my rush to leave the store, I smacked into Mont who was hauling a box of items over to the tourist side. The box slipped from his hands and crashed to the ground, busting open and spilling its contents everywhere.

"I'm sorry," I said, as I bent down to help pick them up.

"S'all right." He grabbed the National Geographic sea monster DVDs, and I got the pile of Little Mermaid story books. He stuck a gnarled pinky finger out from beneath his movies and pointed to my books. "That's the real story, ya know."

"The *real* story?"

"Yep. Disney got it all wrong. If ya want the truth, ask *him*." He indicated Hans Christian Andersen's name on the spines.

I didn't bother telling him the man was long dead, because then Mont would probably tell me he'd spoken to his ghost. I just nodded and said, "Oh, really?" Because I kind of wanted to see where he was going with this. Or maybe I just needed a distraction.

"As I live and breathe," he said, and he crossed his heart and saluted me. Then he leaned in with a secret. "But old Hans didn't know the whole story."

"Which was?" He followed me to the other side of the store, where we began shelving our items.

"That girl may have died, but her sisters didn't." He looked around, surveying the couple passing by the window and eying the corners of the room like he was searching for non-existent security cameras. Then he lowered his voice even more. His wiry eyebrows waggled with importance. "Some of their descendants ended up here in Seal Bay. I bet you know a few if you think about it."

I humored him with a smile. "I always thought there was something fishy about my Oceanography teacher."

He held up one finger, and his mouth hung open while he searched for something else to say. Then he broke into a raspy laugh and winked at me. "Good girl. Now you're seeing with your soul."

At home, I stared out my window, trying not to think about money. We'd make it. We always did. Summer was almost here, and business would pick up then. Tourists. Busy season. Right?

I touched my fingers to the glass, tracing the outline of the horizon—broad and infinite. To take off over the edge would be to leave everything behind. Something I'd thought about . . . more than once. Maybe it was a good thing my dad had sold his boat, because there were times I would have taken a page from Ian's book and gone off to seek my own adventure.

Maybe.

Probably not.

But if I was too scared to chase the horizon, at least I had the seals. No less than two dozen of them lounged on my rocks, posing for me, begging me to let them help us out of this slump. Who was I to argue?

I grabbed my camera and ran down to the water where I snapped tons of photos—close-ups, eyes only, small groups, large groups, swimming, resting—in hopes that I'd find a few good shots to paint. Sometimes, I made the photos into postcards and sold them as well, but the paintings always sold better. I liked to think it's because I put a little bit of myself into them.

Leilani was there, mugging proudly for the camera, right along with the rest of her pod. But there were at least a dozen others there I didn't recognize. I approached a sleek, brown one sunning himself on the lowest rock and sat down beside him. His eyes studied me with an eerie intelligence, and I got the feeling he'd been waiting for me. Owen used to do that.

"What are you guys doing here?" I asked quietly. "Passing through or did you come to stay?"

He swung his head back and forth, surveying the scenery, then settled back down on the rock as if to say, "Here's good."

"It's nice to meet you, then. I'm Aileen. And you are?"

He adjusted his front flippers and snorted. Guess he wasn't ready to tell me yet.

I looked at the way he rested there, so calm and relaxed. I wished I could find that same sort of peace. "Can I tell you something?"

He didn't answer so I plowed on. Some girls had diaries. I had seals.

"Do you know Jamie? He's this guy that swims out here a lot." The seal slapped his tail against the rock as if he knew what I meant. So he was listening at least. "Well, anyway, Jamie scares me sometimes with the way he acts, the things he says. He's hiding something huge, and it confuses me way more than it should. My friend says I shouldn't trust him, and I know she's right, but when I'm with him . . . oh my God. When I'm with him, I want nothing more than to know what kissing him would feel like." Saying it out loud brought a flush to my cheeks, and I ducked my head down into my hands.

The seal snorted again, but didn't do anything else.

"I'm sorry. TMI." And ridiculous to top it off. I had a very good reason for telling Jamie to go away. Maybe I should get an ink pen and write it across my palm so I'd remember for once. "Thanks for listening though. I just need to do what Mae says and forget about him."

His answer was to roll off the rock and into the water. Before I knew it, he was swimming parallel to the beach under our pier and straight toward Jamie's. He looked back once, daring me to follow.

I jumped from the rock and splashed up to the beach, then ran along the shore to catch up with the seal. He stopped and floated in the water, waiting for me. When I reached him, he cut his eyes toward Jamie's house, then back to me.

"What? No! I'm not going there!"

He snorted, as if to say, "Suit yourself." A moment later, he ducked under the water and didn't resurface.

"You're not helping!" I picked up a shell and threw it near where he'd disappeared, then dusted the sand from my hands.

I didn't care. About Jamie's family or his secrets.

I kept repeating that to myself as I trudged back through the dunes, up my porch steps, and into my house where I spent a half hour staring out my window. I didn't care that no one was home again. I didn't care that I wanted to hear Jamie's voice more than anything else in the world. I didn't care. I didn't care. I didn't . . .

*Liar.*

Before I talked myself out of it, I slipped out the back door and headed down the beach to Jamie's house, hoping they weren't on their way back, because I couldn't stop my feet if I wanted to. I gave myself the excuse that I was just checking on Bridget. I needed proof that she was all right, then maybe I could forget about them, stop letting their secrets consume me.

What was their secret anyway? What was he protecting? Mont's voice crept into my mind. He'd tell me Bridget was a mermaid and his family took their boat to Atlantis every night to . . . oh, hell.

I was clearly insane. Only a crazy person would find themselves slinking up the steps to the Flannigan's porch, peeking in their windows, and searching for a giant animated arrow that said, "This is what you're looking for."

Except this wasn't a cartoon, so naturally, all I found was a perfectly normal living room. Two couches, stuffed chairs, family pictures lining their walls, including old black and white ones dating back to the 1800s. No TV just like he'd told me.

If I angled my head a certain way, I could see into their kitchen, and that looked normal too. They had a magnet-covered refrigerator and stained teapot just like in my own house.

I was about to jump off the porch when one of the pictures caught my eye. It looked like it could have been Fee when she was my age, standing next to a really cute guy. He had his arm around her and they both had silly, embarrassed smiles plastered on their faces, the kind you get when you like someone and the adults around you won't let it go. Was it really her? I squinted my eyes to better see the other photos, and sure enough, I saw what looked like a family reunion picture with the same girl and boy sitting on the ground, front and center. Something about that picture rattled in my memory, and I couldn't shake it loose. I'd have to ask her about it later.

With no sign of Bridget in either of those rooms, I made my way around the house, peering through the rest of the windows. On the final side of the house, I found what looked like a teenage girl's bedroom, but it was empty. I let out a relieved breath. They must have taken her to the hospital after all. She would be fine.

With only one window remaining, I should have gone home, but process of elimination told me who belonged inside that room. There was no sign of their boat approaching, so I tiptoed up to the window and peeked in.

The room was sparse, practical, and it reminded me a little bit of Fee's bedroom. She always said, "The only things I need are here and here," while patting her heart and her temple. But I happened to know she kept a chest in the attic full of memories. I wondered if Jamie had something similar.

As I scanned the room I didn't see a chest, but I did spot something that tickled inside of me, a postcard of Owen tucked into Jamie's dresser mirror. It was the same image as the painting he'd been holding in Fish Tales. The painting was probably too expensive for him, but he must have gone back and bought the postcard to remember me, or that day. It didn't surprise me so much that he had bought it, but that he'd kept it. I'd kicked him out of my life. If he'd done that to me, I would have taken any memories of him to my dad's store and fed it through his shredder, twice.

Feeling more confused than ever, I headed back home. Jamie was still thinking about me, and that came very close to thrilling me, even though I had forbidden those feelings. But what if Fee knew them well enough to change things? What if she could answer the questions Jamie wouldn't? When I got home, she was asleep on the couch, so I went into the hallway and pulled on the string to bring the ladder down from the attic. The thought of her chest had nudged a memory, and I wanted to see if I was right.

The only light in the attic came from a bare bulb hanging from a string in the center, so I dragged her chest over beneath it and lifted the lid. Dim shadows fell across its contents: her yellowed wedding dress and a few other clothes, a small white box with her pearls in it, Grandpa Colm's Navy pins, some children's books from the forties and fifties, and a photo album. Whenever I'd visited her as a child, she'd let me play in the chest, but I hadn't looked through it since I'd stopped playing dress up. I pulled out the over-stuffed photo album and set it down on the floor. Tucked somewhere into the middle was the picture I'd been looking for, a large family shot with a girl sitting next to a boy, the two of them front and center. Now that I could see the picture better, I knew it was Fee. Her eyes and her hair were unmistakable. The boy had his arm around her, and she wore what looked like an engagement ring on her finger. I *had* to know more about this.

With the picture pinched under my chin, I climbed back down the ladder. As soon as my sneakers hit the floor, Fee's voice called from another room.

"Did you find what you were looking for?"

I pushed the ladder up into the ceiling and called back, "Yep."

"Wanna share?" she asked. And I knew she wasn't being nosy, just interested.

I found her in the living room and handed her the picture. "This."

"Ah," she said as she studied it. I knew the look on her face, the one that popped up whenever she opened a door to the past. The looks were rare, and the doors always led to unexpected places. "I wondered if this would come up."

I snuggled in beside her. Story time.

She held the picture in both hands, her thumbs on the bottom corners. Her deep, lonely sigh buried itself in my soul. "Quinn and I were to be married that fall. We had grown up together. Our families expected it. And I loved him so much. He—" She coughed away the catch in her voice. "He was a good man. He was Jamie's uncle."

So Jamie and I could have been related? The thought gave me the creeps, and even though I never wanted anything bad to happen to Fee, I was glad she'd ended up with Colm. "But you didn't marry him."

"No." She placed the picture face down on the coffee table. "I ran away to Ireland after . . ."

"After what? What happened?"

She shrugged, but I could see a heaviness in her shoulders like the weight was still there. Fee took my hands in hers and squeezed. "So many things." And the way she spoke, I could tell those "things" were heartbreaking. "I couldn't handle that life anymore."

I ran my thumb over her wedding ring. I knew what had happened in Ireland. She'd met my grandpa. But I needed to know what drove her there. What she meant by "that life."

"I want to know," I said. "Will you tell me?"

She sat up straighter, her burden already lightened by my questions. This was the story she needed to tell, maybe as much as I needed to hear it.

My heart raced as she began.

"The Flannigans are an unusual family. But in many ways they—"

The front door slammed. I jumped and realized I'd been holding my breath.

"I'm home," my mom called down the hallway. "How's frozen lasagna sound?"

"Good," I yelled back over my shoulder. Then I turned back to Fee, anxious for her to continue. She stared pointedly toward the kitchen where Mom was making the oven beep, then shook her head. Another time.

"But is Jamie . . ."

"Every choice has its drawbacks and its benefits," she said while she cranked up the volume on a game show and settled back against the couch. "Just follow your soul."

As the announcer congratulated the winning contestant, she sealed her lips with a knowing smile.

# Chapter Nine

"Look who has a stalker." Mae pointed across the school parking lot to the park on the other side of the road. Jamie sat on a bench a few feet from the sidewalk, feeding bread to the ducks.

"It's a public park," I said with my eyes pinned on him. Ever since I'd spotted my postcard in his room, I'd been hoping to see him. I didn't have the words to actually speak to him, but talking with Fee had made me wonder if I'd made a mistake in pushing him away.

"Something is wrong with his family, Aye. Are you telling me you think he's there by accident?"

"No. I'm not." In fact, when he looked up and his eyes locked on mine, I knew he'd come for me. But no matter what Mae was thinking, his being there was a lot more innocent than me snooping around his house.

I kept my eyes on him as I wove through the lot towards Mae's car. When we got to the edge of the lot, maybe thirty feet away from him, Jamie's face slid into a grin.

I froze, caught between the desire to run to him and my promise to myself I'd stay away. When I thought of how badly I'd failed at the second one, I bounced on my toes. Whatever their secret was, Fee approved of Jamie and his family. Maybe the attacks didn't have anything to do with them. Maybe the two girls had just been in the wrong place at the wrong time. And as much as I'd been trying to deny it, I missed him. I was worried about Bridget, and he was right there. I took a step toward him.

"Hey." Mae grabbed me by the shoulders and flipped me around to face her. "No moping after Stalker Boy. We have plans, remember?"

"But, I . . ." I looked back over my shoulder, and Jamie was gone. I sighed, part relieved and part frustrated. "Yeah. Let's go."

Our plans involved meeting Steven for hamburgers at our town's one and only restaurant. I hadn't wanted to go. The last thing I needed was a reminder of how she had a "true love" boyfriend, while I was once again hopelessly single. But since she begged and pleaded, promising she'd make it up to me with a 7up ice cream float, I agreed to go. Besides, it was better than my own plans, which had been to hang out with the seals and babble to them about the thousand ways Jamie confused me. I'd been doing that all week.

When we got to the diner, I froze in the doorway. Not only was Steven already there, but so was his brother.

"No way!" I said and backed out onto the sidewalk. Ian and I hadn't spoken since that day under the firs and I planned to keep it that way. I was already halfway to the car when Mae caught up with me.

"Come on, Aye." She grabbed my shoulders and forced me to look at her. "It's not a hook-up. I promise."

"I don't care. You know what he said about Jamie."

"Yeah. The same things you said when you were crying to me on the phone after you broke up with him."

Not even close. "He said Jamie's family is weird."

"And you said you didn't trust him. Wanna explain why?"

I got my fingers ready to tick off the reasons, but nothing came out the way it sounded in my head. "Because his family won't . . . Because Bridget isn't . . . Because they . . ."

When my excuses fizzled out, Mae folded her arms across her chest and smiled proudly. "Because they're weird?"

"No." I folded my arms too, but mostly because I was feeling stubborn. "They're just . . . different."

Mae tilted her head in her way that always made me think she saw the world a little cock-eyed. "Differently weird?"

I pressed my lips shut.

"Come on. I don't want to miss hanging out with you because you can't get along with Ian. Can't you at least try?"

I looked over to the diner windows where Ian was watching the two of us. His face was a blank mask. I had no idea what I would meet if I went inside.

"Please?" She poked her finger in the tickly spot in my ribs.

I danced away. "Stop it!"

She continued her attack. "Please. Please. Please. Pleeease. I'll be your best friend."

I held the giggles in as long as I could, but it was hard to stay mad at her. I held up my arms in surrender, mainly to stop the tickling. "Fine! I give up! I'll do it."

Mae threw her arm around me and laughed like she never had any doubt she would win. "That's my girl!"

Right before we got to the door, she stopped. "You're gonna play nice, right?"

"I will if he does."

"That's all I ask." And she pulled me inside.

The boys already had a corner booth. Mae cozied up to Steven, and I slid in on Ian's side. He gave me a look that clearly said he and Steven just had the same conversation Mae and I had in the parking lot.

I stayed close to the booth's edge, keeping a respectable amount of the red, cushioned seat between us. Apparently that wasn't enough, because he scooted a little closer to the wall and began picking at the torn, vinyl corners of his menu. *Alrighty then.* I looked to Mae, who shrugged before gesturing to the waitress that we were ready.

Once the menus were gone, and Ian no longer had anything to fiddle with, he directed his gaze out the window. Mae didn't notice, because she was too absorbed in Steven, but I noticed enough for everyone. Everything about him, from the strong, unyielding line of his jaw to the way his hand kept clenching and unclenching, told me he shared my feeling of wanting to be anywhere else on the planet.

How long until the food got here and we could leave? Twenty minutes? Thirty?

After an excruciatingly long time with Ian tapping his foot on the floor, our drinks arrived. He wrapped his hand around his soda and pulled it closer to him. Away from me.

I refused to sit through the entire meal like this, so I took a sip for courage and asked Ian, "Can we end this?"

"I don't know. Can we?" he said to the window.

"Okay, fine." If you're gonna be that way . . .

"Just ignore him," Steven said. "He's been acting this way ever since last night."

Mae put her elbow on the table and her chin in her hand and blinked enthusiastically at Steven. "Oooh, what happened?"

"Hansel and Rowe stopped by again."

"They did?" I asked.

Ian slammed his palm down on the table and faced me for the first time today. The fire in his eyes made me wish he hadn't. "Yeah. So what if I hung out with that girl once? So what if I went hiking near her house the weekend she disappeared? How was I supposed to know where she lived? She never told me that. I'm sick of getting hounded because of your boyfriend's family. Dad refuses to talk—"

"He's not her boyfriend," Mae said.

"—about it and I'm guessing you know more than you're telling and . . . I . . . she . . . what?"

"She dumped him," Mae said simply.

"You did?" he asked, his anger softening into surprise.

"Yeah, um . . ." I said into my drink. I hadn't expected the conversation to take this turn, and I didn't like that everyone at the table now knew about my failed love life. I glared at Mae. I should have known she wouldn't keep her mouth shut. While she tried to look guilty, Ian and Steven stared at me, waiting for an explanation, so I added, "It was sort of a trust thing." I neglected to mention how much I wanted to undo it.

"I'm sorry." Ian relaxed enough to not be hugging the wall anymore. "I didn't know. It's just, my dad says to trust him, but he won't tell me anything. And I thought maybe you were hiding something because . . ." He waved his hand at me, then let it flop back on the table.

"I'm not," I said. "I promise." He looked so miserable that I might have reached out to touch his arm, if we'd been the kind of friends that did that sort of thing. "And I'm sorry too, that they won't leave you alone." As I said it, I realized it was the absolute truth. I'd been angry at him before, because he had been accusing Jamie's family of something I hadn't wanted to hear. Well, I should have reacted better. While I still couldn't believe Jamie's family had anything to do with the deaths, the truth was I had known Ian most of my life. He liked to challenge the rules, but I'd never known him to get into a fight or to hurt anyone physically. I only wanted to blame him because he hurt my feelings in eighth grade. Maybe I wasn't entirely over that, but the least I could do was offer him my friendship. He looked like he needed it. "I wish there was something I could do."

Ian shrugged, pushing all of his frustrations away with that motion, and smiled. It was the first smile he'd given me since the night of the party, and I was relieved to see it. He took a breath like he wanted to say something else, but his brother interrupted him.

"I'm glad you asked." Steven pulled a folded sheet of paper from his pocket, which he then passed across the table to me.

"What's this?" I asked, picking it up and turning it in my fingers.

Ian nudged me with his elbow, keeping part of his arm pressed against mine as he scooted closer. Huh. Maybe he *was* that kind of friend. "Open it."

Inside, I found a printout of a partial email. Mae got on her knees and leaned halfway across the table so she could read it along with me.

*To: rdthornton*

*Subject: Re: The Flannigans*

*I've been combing through the Flannigan's case file. There has to be some hint in there as to their hiding places. A pattern or something. Once I figure that out, I'll make sure I'm there first. I'll be*

"I'll be what?" I asked flipping the paper over and back, hoping more words would suddenly appear. "Where's the rest of it?"

Stephen said, "That's all there was. Dad got interrupted while he was typing it."

I followed Stephen's gaze to his brother. "Interrupted?"

Ian relaxed against the seat, his arm casually thrown across the back. "There may have been a small fire in the kitchen."

"Our dad doesn't like to keep records," Steven clarified. "If we wanted to find anything, we had to do it that way. In fact, I went back to check after he had gone to bed to see if I could find anything else, and that message along with any others had been deleted. No emails. No files, electronic or otherwise. Nothing."

"Well, who's R D Thornton?" I asked.

Ian spoke up. "Some government guy, but I am not starting a fire in his office. Even our dad wouldn't be able to get me out of that one."

I laughed. I liked the funny, easy-going Ian. I'd forgotten how much fun we used to have together when we were younger.

Mae leaned across the table and lowered her voice like she was in some reality show about spies. Then again, she probably thought she was. "I think the Flannigans are drug dealers. And oh! Maybe they're part of a mob, and if anyone in the family tries to get away, they're punished."

Ignoring her, I turned to Steven. "What do you think it means?"

He shrugged. "I don't know, but if it's important enough to delete, then it's important enough to worry about."

"How does your dad know all of this stuff?" I asked, remembering his smile at the town meeting when everyone seemed to forget about the murder. "How exactly is he involved? Do you think he's *responsible* in some way?"

"No," Steven said. "Our dad's a prosecuting attorney, and he only handles the big stuff. He wouldn't have a case file on the Flannigans unless they were serial killers or major drug traffickers or something."

Ian nodded in agreement. "There's definitely something going on with them that no one is supposed to know about. And I'm willing to bet if we find out what, then my name will be cleared."

"But what is it?" I said, more to myself than to anyone there. *Jamie, what's going on?*

"Maybe we shouldn't be talking about this here," Mae whispered. "Maybe we should make up code words for—"

"All right," the waitress arrived at our table with a large oval tray balanced on her shoulder. "I've got a hamburger. No pickles, extra cheese."

"That'd be me," Steven said.

She passed out the rest of the orders and left. Thankfully, the food silenced everyone, sparing me more of Mae's theatrics and giving me time to think about that email. A pattern to their hiding places. Is that where they went in that little rowboat? To hide things? Mae's insanity aside, the only thing that made sense was drugs. And I wished to God that it didn't make sense.

I stayed quiet for the rest of our meal and for the ride home. In my driveway, Mae shifted her car into park and turned to me, any hint of conspiracy gone from her face. "Look, I don't know what the deal is with Jamie's family, but I think you should listen to the boys. Something's not right, and I'm worried about you."

"So am I." But it wasn't for the reasons Mae gave. I was worried because even though I'd heard the warnings, and seen the email, and had confirmation from Jamie himself they were somehow involved in something bad, I couldn't let it go. I felt like I was tangled up in the giant fishing net of their lives. I couldn't free myself, and I didn't want to. The only thing to do now was to ensnare myself further, swim deeper, and hope I didn't drown.

Mom had a rare day off and had plopped herself in the living room next to Fee, so I headed for my bedroom. I had paintings to finish and final exams to study for, but I spent the majority of the evening sitting on my window seat and staring out at the water. It could have been just me and the fact that I'd been taking Mae's crazy pills lately, but the pull of the ocean seemed to get stronger, dragging me deeper and deeper into its gravity. The sun set, and as the blue water turned silver and then black, I imagined myself diving in and splashing through the waves. More than that, I imagined I *could*. Goosebumps appeared on my arms as I thought of the cool, crisp water supporting me, washing over me.

I spotted him ducking under a wave a few feet out—my seal as I'd come to call him. He emerged from the water and disappeared behind a rock on the beach. And suddenly, I had to see him. I jumped out the window, because if I cut through the living room and Mom caught me, she'd forbid me from going out there alone at night. I ran to the spot where he'd disappeared, but I saw nothing there. Not even a trail in the sand where he had wiggled through. I looked up and down the beach. Still nothing.

No, wait.

A light flickered on by Jamie's porch door, and he stepped inside. Where had he been? Swimming? It looked like he was wearing his swimsuit, so maybe he had.

And maybe, just before the lights went out, I saw him peering through the sliding glass door and smiling at me.

# Chapter Ten

Dad had to make a large delivery to a customer up in Astoria, so he asked if I'd help at Fish Tales after school. Deliveries, especially at that distance, brought in extra money, so of course I agreed. He even sweetened the deal by promising I wouldn't have to touch a single piece of bait. Mont would do that while I ran the register and re-stocked the tourist side.

Bribery. It was rarely necessary (from my dad at least) but always welcome.

The prospect of more money coming in made my feet a lot lighter, inspiring me to dance and twirl my way through the afternoon, singing along to the old, static-clogged radio we had duct-taped to the wall by the bait cooler. It was the only spot in the entire store that got reception. Mont laughed and occasionally danced with me, but his bad knee kept him from going too wild.

It was a slow day, like too many of them lately, but I sold a couple of paintings which added a small chunk to my "Save the Store" fund. And Mont booked a fishing trip, which we celebrated by clinking our soda cans together and downing a mouthful of M&M's. I knew he struggled with his bills as much as we did, but like Dad, he pushed forward to the next day, hoping for things to get better.

Towards evening, when the trickle of customers cut off altogether, Mont and I settled onto the wooden stools behind the register. It had been a tradition of ours ever since I could remember where he'd tell me stories to pass the empty minutes before seven o'clock when we officially shut the doors. I'd heard them all a dozen times at this point, my favorite being the one that named him. He told anyone who'd listen that a nereid helped him during a storm in Montreal. According to him, that was when he started going by Mont, so he'd never forget. It's also why he repeated the stories so often, because "they get lost when you're silent."

He placed his right foot on the bottom rung of the stool, then grabbed his left leg with both hands and hoisted it up, grunting as he did so. "Damn selkies. Next time, I'll give 'em what for."

I giggled, picturing him standing on the docks, waving his fist in the air, while little seals bobbed in the water, wondering what they did wrong. "Oh, come on. They can't be all bad."

"Now you listen up, little one." He shook his finger at me. "Those selkies ain't like the seals you paint. They's soulless creatures, and they bring nothing but heartache. The proof is in the way you call em."

"Call them? How?" I tried to picture a seal holding a cell phone and laughed.

"Pain." He growled the word, the sound rumbling through his chest.

I stopped laughing as his eyes swirled into the most intense blue I'd ever seen. When I thought of pain, one image came to mind. I sat up straight in my seat. "Wh— what kind of pain?" Blood? Skin?

Sacrifice of a teenage girl?

He held up both hands, raising each finger one by one, until he got to the seventh. He rasped out the answer. "Seven teardrops into the ocean."

"Teardrops?" That's it? I puffed out a breath and relaxed. What was with me lately? Listening to Mae's conspiracy theories and Mont's daydreams. I had cried tons of times into the ocean, and no one had ever came running.

Except for Jamie. His family may have been odd, but they couldn't be mythical sea creatures. They were nice, normal . . . Well, they had a secret, but it wasn't that.

"You okay, little one? You look a bit spooked."

Voices floated through my head, nudging my thoughts into a place that shouldn't exist.

*I couldn't handle that life anymore.*

No. I shook my head, refusing to let the idea have weight, but those voices were stubborn.

*They're an unusual family,* which led to, *I'm protecting everyone in my family.*

No. Stop it!

*Hiding places . . .*

No! I couldn't possibly be entertaining those thoughts.

I shuffled through my mind for the facts, solid proof that they were normal. But the only things I could think of were as liquid as, well, water. They were a family who didn't stay in one place. Horrible things happened to them, but they wouldn't go to any doctors or the police. And Jamie had a huge secret that he couldn't share with me.

"How do you know about the tears?" I asked carefully.

"How else?" He pointed to the tourist side of the shop where the books I'd stocked earlier sat on the shelf. *Sea Myths and Legends. Selkies and Roanes. Our Magical Seas.*

"Those are just stories the tourists want to hear," I said stubbornly. "None of that's real."

He tapped the side of his head. "My memories are real. What about yours? You remember, don't you?"

I didn't have to ask what he meant. "The accident." I'd been pushing those memories away for so long, they'd twisted into imaginings, just like Mont's stories. But he knew about them. I used to talk about them constantly, until I got older and my mom told me to stop being ridiculous. I slipped down off the stool, gripping the edge of the counter to steady myself. "I . . . I need to . . ." I flicked my eyes wildly around the shop, trying to figure out what exactly I needed to do. I looked to Mont for help.

"Go," he said. "I understand what it's like when a new world opens up."

My heart raced and my mind spun as I retrieved my backpack from the office.

"Don't forget this. It's good research." He tucked *Selkies and Roanes* into my bag, and I numbly made my way out the door.

At home, alone, I cracked open the book. The first legend was one I'd heard at least a dozen times.

Many years ago, a fisherman watched a seal crawl into a cave, then gaped in awe as a beautiful girl emerged. Curious, the fisherman searched the cave where he found a seal skin hidden among the rocks. He realized the woman was a selkie, a seal with the ability to shift into human form, and he knew if he captured the skin, she would forever belong to him. So, he hid the skin in his own secret spot, and the woman agreed to be his wife. She bore his children, and one day, her youngest daughter found a seal skin buried in a chest in the woods. With her skin returned to her, the woman gathered her children and took them with her into the ocean. He followed them, only to be captured by her family and tortured until he promised to never seek them out again.

Mont's story to the letter.

Another one told of a lonely housewife, who was lured away from her family by a selkie male's charm. After she pledged her love to him, he shunned her, returning to the sea. Still under his spell, she followed him, drowning herself rather than return to her loving family.

I paged through a few more stories, but it was more of the same: selkies portrayed as devilish creatures, fairy tales written by imaginative sailors after too much time at sea. Chucking it across the room, I got up and slipped out my window. Fairy tales weren't going to help me sort things out. I needed the truth. I needed *him*.

During the short walk to his house, puzzle pieces shifted around in my mind, clicking into place to form a picture I had never thought to imagine. Yet somehow, I knew it was right. I had an attachment to the ocean, and to him. They had to be linked.

I didn't have to knock. Maybe he saw me coming, or maybe he just felt it, but he slipped out his back door the second I stepped on to his porch, wearing his trademark tour t-shirt and swim suit.

"Let's talk," I said, gesturing toward the beach. I needed to ground myself in the water or else I wouldn't be able to speak at all.

He nodded, and we walked. The sun had already set, and the stars were slowly sparking into existence.

With my flip-flops dangling from my fingers, and my feet squishing into the wet sand, I began. "When I was three years old, I was washed overboard during a storm, and I was rescued by seals."

His eyes squinched up and he said, "I thought you said your grandmother rescued you."

"She did, three days later. My family always said they didn't know what happened to me during that time, that what I remembered was a result of the shock from a traumatic accident."

"And what do you remember?"

I sifted through the fuzzy memories, trying to place them in an order that made sense. I hadn't accessed them for so long, I couldn't be sure what was real and what wasn't, but there were a few things that still felt solid and true. "Riding on the back of a seal. Not afraid, but exhilarated . . . free. He took me to an island with a large cave, where a number of seals spent their days. There were humans there too, who fed me and took care of me. They fussed over me like I was their own child, braiding my hair and playing with my toes."

"That doesn't sound too bad."

"But you can understand why my mom made me stop talking about it, right? I mean, a family living in a cave with seals. It sounds a little crazy."

"Not *that* crazy."

"No," I said thoughtfully. "I don't suppose *you'd* think so." I stopped walking, and we faced each other. His eyes locked with mine, huge and brown and deeper than any ocean. "Well, what about this? When I'd lie there at night, somewhere between sleep and awake, I'd imagine the people changing. Magic rippling around their bodies as they became something else. Something any normal person would shrug off as a dream."

He didn't laugh. Or argue. Or walk away. In fact, he gave me that same knowing smile I often saw on Fee. "But it wasn't a dream."

I breathed a sigh of relief. I hadn't realized how badly I needed to hear that. I licked my lips and pressed on. "You stay away from doctors, from people in general. You're always swimming in the middle of the night, or off with your family in that boat. All of those seals came to Deirdre's memorial. I cried into the ocean and you . . ." I stopped, because that part still seemed a little strange. "You disappear, and all I can find is a seal. Or the opposite. I watch a seal crawl away, and then I see you smiling at me." He took a step forward. My hand reached out and hovered over his chest. Was it just me, or was there magic radiating from him? "Are . . . are you?"

He closed the distance. My hand touched him, and I felt his heart racing beneath my fingers. "Go ahead. Ask it."

Common sense threatened to burst through, telling me to swallow the words and rethink this whole thing before he confirmed my insanity. I told that part of me to shut up and put my other hand on his chest. We both stopped breathing, and with a whisper that echoed through the night, I asked, "Are you a selkie?"

His fingers closed around mine. "Yes."

# Chapter Eleven

"Why didn't you tell me?" I asked, my feet swishing through the water. As soon as Jamie had confirmed my suspicions, he'd taken my hand and led me to my rocks which provided us with a little privacy, not that anyone else was out there.

"I'm not supposed to tell anyone," he said, though he seemed relieved I knew.

"But since I guessed?"

"It's time you knew anyway. I never wanted to lie to you about it."

"Then why did you?" I asked softly. I didn't blame him, because that's not something you go around blabbing. I just wanted to hear his answer.

"Because not all secrets are mine to tell." His eyes flashed with something I couldn't identify. The Shadow again. I wondered how many of those he carried within him.

Well, now that he was talking, I was going to ask. There was so much more I needed to know. "What is it, Jamie?"

He threaded his fingers through mine, squeezing like he was drawing strength from me. "Deirdre and Bridget were attacked for the same reason." He looked at me, and his eyes melted with pain. "Someone's hunting us."

"Hunting?" I wanted to make sure I'd heard it right, but the grotesque images flashing through my mind confirmed that I had.

Deirdre floating in the ocean, her body bloated and unrecognizable. Bridget screaming while someone attacked her, so close to safety, and so afraid. The flash of a knife blade. An attacker, huge and imposing stalking closer and closer. I blinked the images away, unable to handle them. "Who's doing this?"

"We don't know. Bridget didn't see who attacked her." His face was a mixture of fury and determination, the relentless drive of the sea given form. "That's why we go out every night. We have to find them and stop them."

"Why would someone do that?"

"My sister had her skin in a cave. She told Kyle she wanted to show him a secret. She had some crazy idea that she could transform in front of him, and he would fall madly in love with her. They'd planned to meet in the cave."

"But Kyle wasn't there."

Jamie shook his head. "While she was pulling her skin out of a hole, someone attacked her from behind."

"Oh my God." The horrifying image of her came back as he replayed that night. Her face. Her stomach.

"He sliced her open so she couldn't fight back and left her for dead," he said through gritted teeth. "He stole her skin, and if she doesn't get it back, the injuries will kill her. My uncle stitched her up, and we have a limited supply of medicine. For now, she's stable and in a safe place, but she needs to transform if she's ever going to get better."

"Why is that?"

"Our skins contain healing properties."

"Is that why the hunters want them?"

He growled, like the answer sickened him. "Some people want the trophy, proof that we exist. But most people want to sell them. The buyers wouldn't be able to turn into selkies themselves, but there are people out there who've found a way to harness the magic. To use the healing properties to extend their lives for years, decades." He picked up a rock, stared at it for a moment with distant eyes, then hurled it into the water. Maybe I didn't want to know the rest. This was all too much, as evidenced by Jamie's strained voice. "They grind the skins into a powder, which they use to create lotions, vitamins, whatever they can think of, and sell them over the internet to the highest bidder."

I shuddered. Bridget needed her skin to heal herself, but some obscenely rich person had no problem sacrificing her for their own gain. "Do you think her boyfriend had something to do with it? He's the only one who knew she'd be there, right?"

"No. Kyle texted her later that night, complaining about getting called back to work. Bridget confirmed it with someone he worked with." Jamie gave a short, harsh laugh. "He's lucky I was the one sitting with her when the text came through. If it had been my dad, he would have tracked Kyle down and punched him senseless."

I tried to imagine Jamie's dad punching anyone like that. He'd been so nice to me, but I saw how angry he got at the bonfire. He was a big man. I supposed he'd be capable of just about anything if it concerned his family. "Then who do you think it was?"

"It could be anyone. If they knew about us, all they had to do was wait for someone to lead them to one of our hiding places."

"Mr. Glenn!" His name popped out of my mouth. I was right before. I never should have discounted him.

"Who's he?"

"My friends' dad." Stephen said it couldn't be him, but knowing what I did now, his dad was the only possible suspect. The phone call. The email. "He has a case file on you guys, and he said he's looking for hiding places."

Jamie jumped to his feet, his eyes alive with renewed energy. "This could be it. I've got to tell my dad."

"I'll talk to my friend."

"Great. Let me know what you find out." He had only gone a few steps before he turned back around. "Hey, I know my life is crazy, not just now, but all the time. I still have to ask. Do you want to go on a date with me?"

Whiplash. I had whiplash from the sudden change of subject. I wanted to tell him that, but before the words could form, I realized it wasn't so sudden after all. Change was coming. I could feel it not only from him, but from the air around us. Better days and carefree nights. And the promise of Jamie by my side. "Yes. I do."

He nodded, a small, relieved motion as if I'd ever say no. "Saturday, then?"

"Saturday."

As he disappeared into the night, I leaned back against the rock, my heart pumping in excited little beats, ready for what was to come.

# Chapter Twelve

I climbed into Ian's car; black and sleek and smelling of new leather.

"Thanks for letting me come over," I said. When I'd found him at lunch, he hadn't questioned why I suddenly wanted to hang out. And I hadn't volunteered the reason. Telling your friend his dad is responsible for murdering fairy tale characters is not something you do over cold meatloaf and tater tots. But when was the perfect time to tell him? It didn't seem like a car conversation either.

"No problem." He drummed his fingers on his steering wheel, then started fiddling with some buttons on his phone. "You like music?"

"Sure."

He loaded up something and pumped it through speakers that probably cost more than my dad's truck, brand new. Then he looked to me like he was waiting for my approval.

"That's good," I said, mostly because it didn't matter. I had too much on my mind to worry about song choice.

"Cool," he mumbled.

For the rest of the drive, Ian didn't say much. He stared through the windshield and kept his hands wrapped around the steering wheel. I was about to ask if he was mad at me again, but by then we were pulling up in front of his house.

Well, mansion, would be a better word. It sat on top of a secluded hill, not far from the marina, but with enough trees that they didn't have to stare at us riff-raff from their balconies. All three of them.

Ian offered the grand tour of his house, and I accepted. It was the best way to snoop around without actually snooping. Plus, I really wanted to see their house. When we were kids, they'd lived in a smaller house in town. That was the one I'd always gone to for birthday parties and stuff. But then Mr. Glenn's law firm grew into one of the most recognized ones in the state, and they traded up. Well, I used to think the firm's success was the reason. Maybe it wasn't.

From the moment we stepped into the house, my jaw was stuck in a permanent down position. Compared to my house . . . well, there was no comparing it to mine. Compared to the museums I'd seen on field trips, it was still the biggest, fanciest building I'd ever been in: shiny, tile floors, humongous portraits lining the walls, and statues dominating corners or displayed on specially built tables. Even though Ian didn't specifically state it, I was pretty sure those bathroom faucets were plated in gold. No Popsicle stick boats or light house lamps in this house.

No evidence of selkie-hunting either, although we never seemed to pass by his dad's office. If I were a crazy, illegal hunter, I would make sure my wares were kept behind locked doors, and from what the boys said, the office was the most forbidden room in the house.

"So," Ian said, once we made it to the kitchen where he offered me a soda and chips, "what did you want to do? We could hang out in the game room . . . play video games, shoot some pool."

"Is your dad home?"

His face crinkled in confusion. "Well, I didn't think you'd want to . . . I mean, if you want privacy, that's not a problem."

"Um . . ." Now I was the one confused. "I'm just asking to see your dad's office. You and Steven found something there about Jamie's family. I wanted to see if we could find more."

"So you didn't . . . no, of course not." His smile faded, shifted into something too quick to define, then was replaced by a frown. "I didn't peg you for a breaking and entering type of girl. Then again, that's why you wanted me, isn't it?"

"Oh." I got it. He didn't know Jamie and I had gotten back together. He thought we were on a date. Suddenly, I felt terrible. "Look, I'm sorry. I didn't mean to—"

He held up a hand to stop me. "Never mind. Let's do it."

He pulled a small metal tool from his pocket knife and had the office door open in less time than it would have taken me if I had a key. Then he waved me in with a flourish. "After you."

"Thanks," I said, surveying the room. It was easily the most sparse room in the house. It was small, about the size of a walk-in closet. One wall was mostly windows, looking out onto the cliff and across the ocean. It was pretty late in the day, and the sun, hanging low over the water, nearly blinded me. Ian picked up a remote control from the desk and pushed one of the buttons. A flap opened in the ceiling just over the windows, and a set of thick, wooden blinds descended, darkening the room. Ian hit another button, and a lamp on the desk flickered on. One wire lay across the sturdy wooden desk, most likely the power cord for a laptop that wasn't there.

There was one wall reserved for floor to ceiling bookcases. I ran my fingers over a few of the spines. Most were law books. The other walls were covered with family pictures and artwork apparently done by Ian and Steven when they were much younger.

"This was from my cubism period." Ian pointed to a framed painting of his family, done in primary colors, where every member of the family had square heads.

"Nice work," I said admiringly. "You should apply to art school."

He shrugged. "Not a chance. You should though."

"Thanks." Again, he surprised me. I had no idea he'd ever seen my paintings. And again, I felt guilty for misleading him. "Look, I'm really sorry that—"

"Like I said, there's nothing in here." He lifted up a few of the paintings, showing me bare walls underneath. "We've checked under every frame. We've moved every book. The shelves are built into the walls, and there's a bathroom directly on the other side, so there can't be anything behind them. We've searched through the desk, even the locked drawers." I looked and, sure enough, there were a couple of drawers that had electronic keypads on them. "I don't know what you think you're gonna find, but get busy. He'll be home soon, and we don't want to be caught in here. Remember what he did when Steven and I took the boat."

"Understood."

Ian left to keep watch from a window at the front of the house, leaving me alone to search. I started with the desk. Ian had scribbled down the codes for me, but after I'd sifted through about thirty folders of trial documents, I moved on to the bookcases. Ian hadn't mentioned anything about searching through the books, and I'd seen enough movies to know that they're prime real estate for secrets. I pulled out several stacks of books and started leafing through them. I'd gotten through about a quarter of the shelves, and had stacks of books strewn all over the floor, when I heard Ian's voice.

"Finish up! Dad just turned onto the driveway!"

Oh, no! My hands shook as I grabbed the closest pile of books and started shoving them back in place. A couple of them slid back onto the floor, dragging half the shelf along with them. Shoot! When did I become such a klutz?

"Aileen!"

I scrambled to pick the books back up. A few of them had fallen open, and a battered piece of paper came fluttering out. I picked it up. It was dated 1965, followed by a list of half a dozen names: Quinn Flannigan, Molly Murray, Fiona Flannigan—

Ian ran into the room. "He's in the garage. We have to go now!"

I stuffed the paper in my pocket, and the two of us crammed the rest of the books onto the shelves. Never mind if they were in the right order, because we could hear Mr. Glenn's footsteps echoing up the stairs.

"Ian, you home?" he called. "I saw your car."

We finished up, locked the door, and ran down the hall into the game room just in time to grab the TV remote and throw ourselves onto the futon. A second later, the door opened.

Mr. Glenn took one look at us sprawled out on the futon, out of breath and probably a little flushed. "Sorry, guys," he said, and shut the door. Then, from the hallway, he shouted, "Use a condom!"

Ian and I sunk back into the cushions. He covered his fire red face with his hands, and I burst into a round of embarrassed giggles.

# Chapter Thirteen

Just before dawn, Fee wheeled into the kitchen where I was sitting at the table clutching a mostly-full cup of coffee. I hadn't slept at all, so I'd gotten up and made myself a pot, because that's what Mom always did to clear out the cobwebs. Of the list of names, I'd only recognized Quinn Flannigan, the man Fee was engaged to before she met Colm. The rest of the names had meant nothing to Jamie or me, and Jamie told me when he'd mentioned Mr. Glenn and the list to his dad, his dad had simply said thanks and he'd take care of it. Did that mean their problems were over? Or did it just mean that we should stay out of it? That was probably the smartest thing to do. The less attention Jamie drew to himself, the better. The last thing I wanted was for anyone else to end up like his sister.

At least I had our date to cheer me up. Maybe. If I could talk my mom into it. That was an entirely different mountain to climb.

I took another sip of coffee and scrunched up my face. The idea of a nice wake-up drink had sounded good, but it tasted like our garbage can smelled.

Laughing, Fee took my mug, dumped half of it in the sink, filled it with an obscene amount of milk and sugar, and handed it back to me.

I sipped, then guzzled the entire thing before I set it down again. "Huge improvement. Thanks."

She scooted up beside me. "Why are you up so early?"

I hadn't seen the dark side of a Saturday morning since I was maybe two, so I could understand her concern. In fact, I was counting on it. I pulled *Selkies and Roanes* from my lap and plopped it on the table.

She eyed it, then me, as if she knew this talk was coming. "How much do you know?"

"Not as much as you, apparently," I said, thumbing through the book. I'd read every last word of it, and it still didn't tell me enough. Like, how do you tell your best friend your boyfriend's a selkie? "Tell me about Jamie's grandfather. Did your parents know he was a selkie?"

"They did."

"How did you tell them?" I could imagine telling my mom. I could also imagine her flipping out and installing steel bars on my window. With alarms. And maybe some pest repellant.

"You forget where my parents came from." She tapped the cover of the book. It had a drawing of a dark-haired girl with magic sparkles surrounding her, and behind her was a map of Ireland. "Back home, people still have faith in the old stories."

"Oh." Neither I nor my mother had ever been there. I'd probably love it. Mom would probably hate it. "Does Mom know about the Flannigans?"

"Puh," Fee huffed. "She knows *of* the Flannigans. They've been coming and going from Seal Bay for over a hundred years, fishing and trading to make the bills. But she doesn't know what they are. They weren't around much when she was a child, and at the time I didn't feel like dredging up old stories."

"So she doesn't know about Quinn either?"

She shook her head; her long, gray braid flipped over her shoulder. "To her, your grandfather was the perfect man. I could never destroy the image of her father being my one and only Prince Charming."

I didn't remember much about my Grandpa Colm, but I did remember the pure joy I felt whenever I was around him, and I knew he was an amazing person. I couldn't blame Fee for not wanting to destroy that image for my mom. "Well, I'm glad you told me."

"I have no secrets from you, little one."

That was true, but sometimes she waited for me to ask the question. That way she always knew I was ready to hear the answer. "What made you leave?"

She shrugged. "The sea didn't call to me anymore. Someone on land did."

"But you didn't meet Grandpa Colm until you got to Ireland."

"I knew he was there, waiting for me, like the other half of my soul."

I thought I understood what she meant. That pull I'd felt my entire life. What if it wasn't the sea calling to me? What if it was Jamie? Was he the other half of my soul? I had never believed in soul mates, but until two days ago I hadn't believed in selkies either. Maybe there was a whole lot more out there waiting for the right person to come along and discover it.

"What are you two conspiring to do now?" Mom shuffled into the kitchen, tightening her "yummy sushi" robe around her waist, then running her hands back through her bed hair.

Fee and I looked at each other, and she gave me an infinitesimal shake of the head. Like I needed her to do that.

"Nothing," I said as Fee slid the book off the table and onto her lap. I popped up and retrieved the milk from the fridge and a box of cereal from the cabinet. Then I poured Mom a cup of coffee, wondering how her taste buds let her drink that stuff black.

"Uh huh." Mom pulled a stack of bowls and some spoons from the dish rack and dropped them in the middle of the table before sinking into her chair. She never had the energy before her Corn Pops to argue.

"Good morning!" Dad, on the other hand, welcomed mornings like most people welcomed oxygen. He squeezed each of our shoulders, and kissed Mom on the top of her head as he circled the table to his seat. "How are my three favorite girls in the entire world?"

Fee and I both said, "Good."

Mom mmphed, and Dad squeezed her hand. "Cheer up, sunshine. Today's gonna be a good day. I can feel it in my bones."

Mom sat up a little straighter, meaning her forehead was no longer on the table. "Have you found out a way to . . ." She looked at me and cut off her words. "To solve that problem we were talking about?"

That problem. Their code for money. I'd figured it out when I was eight, but except for occasionally slipping Dad my earnings, I played dumb, because I knew they'd feel bad if I didn't.

Fee on the other hand . . . "So are you going to sell the store or not?"

"Mom!" My mother slammed her coffee cup down on the table, sloshing the liquid all over her place mat.

"I'm sorry, but you keep enough things from your daughter. She has a right to know what's coming."

"Dad?" He was actually considering selling his store? *Our* store?

"It's okay, sweetie." Dad tucked a piece of my hair behind my ear. "And your mother's right, Ciara. We should have told Aileen long ago. She's not a baby anymore."

Mom flopped back in her chair and sighed. "Fine. So tell us. What's going on?"

"Well," Dad said as he put down his spoon and clasped his hands in front of him on the table. "I've got an idea that I'm pretty sure will get us some money. I'm gonna head out early today and see if I can work on it."

"What is it?" my mom and I asked at the same time. We looked at each other and almost smiled.

"Nope." Dad zipped his lips with his fingers. "I can't talk about it yet. I might jinx it." He may not have fished in thirteen years, but he still held on to the beliefs that ruled the ocean. When it came to sailors and their superstitions, no one could budge him. Never whistle anywhere on a ship. Never step on board with your left foot first. And never talk about the catch before it's caught.

"Are you sure?" Mom arched her eyebrow at my dad. "Because if we have to take out another mortgage on the house—"

"Stop. I wouldn't have said anything if I wasn't positive." Dad touched her shoulder and gently tugged her close enough to kiss her forehead. "We'll have the money by the end of the month. I promise."

"Well, if you promise . . ."

"I do. No more worries." He brushed her hair out of her face and kissed her on the mouth this time.

At his touch, the tension slowly sank out of Mom. "All right then."

I felt a little knot release inside me as well. If Dad said he had a plan, then he did, and he would fix things.

"So, what are you two doing today?" Dad asked both Fee and me, probably to change the subject to a happier topic. "Hanging out together?"

"No, um . . ." I peered inside Mom's coffee cup to see if she'd drank enough ambition to argue. Hopefully not. "I sort of have a date."

Mom sat up straight, her eyes wide. Dangit, I was too late. "With that boy down the beach?" she asked.

"Yes, ma'am."

She sucked down another gulp of coffee. "What are you doing, and will his parents be there?"

Seriously? "He's taking me on a picnic, and please don't tell me you expect us to have a chaperone every time we go out."

"Well, they never caught the person who killed that girl in the bay." Of course she was still dwelling on that.

"Mom," I said reasonably, "Officer Rowe said it was an isolated incident." Yes, I knew differently, but there was no reason to tell her that. "And besides, I'll be back before dark."

"She's right, Ciara," Fee chimed in. "Don't be so overprotective. Let her be a teenager."

I gave Fee a nod of thanks. From the look on her face, she had guessed what happened to Deirdre, but she also knew I was completely safe from that particular danger.

Mom narrowed her eyes at me, and I had to hold back my smile. I knew that look well. She was about to give in, but not without one last ditch effort. "I thought you decided he was stupid."

I shrugged and smiled innocently. "I changed my mind."

Mom dunked a few of her Corn Pops and watched them pop back up. "What do you think, Alex?"

Dad smiled. Small dots of milk hung off the bottom of his mustache. "I think my little girl has herself a boyfriend."

# Chapter Fourteen

Our first stop was the gas station. Jamie and I popped in the little convenience store where he pulled a couple of magazines from the rack at the front.

"You read Cosmo?" I said, eying the covers.

He gave me a "Don't be ridiculous" look and said, "It's for my sister."

"Uh huh. Sure it is."

He shook his head and walked over to the cooler. I was still giggling while we picked out a couple of pre-made sandwiches and some drinks.

"7up, right?" he asked while grabbing a Dr. Pepper for himself.

"My favorite."

"I know." I stopped giggling at the look he gave me, and started blushing.

That warm feeling, however, was cut short when the front door swung open and the cashier shouted out, "Hey, Ben!"

I cringed at the name.

"Chuck!" The shark sidled up to the counter, his grin blaring full force. Jamie and I stood by the refrigerator cases, watching as he vigorously shook hands with the cashier. Was he besties with everyone in town now? He pulled his wallet out and handed over a couple of twenties. "Pump two."

Chuck rang up the sale, and the cash register drawer popped open.

Ben leaned casually against the counter, throwing a wink my way before addressing his BFF. "So how are Marie and the kids?"

"Great." Chuck counted out some bills. "Hey, Marie's sister has been asking about you. Wants to know if you're single."

Ew, disgusting.

Ben beamed. "Aw, you tell your sister-in-law thanks for the compliment, but I'm married to my work."

"I understand that one. There isn't a day goes by my wife doesn't ask me to work less hours. How's your store coming by the way?"

"Good. Good. I'm planning a grand opening this fall."

This fall? Okay, that was enough nonsense. I marched up the counter. Jamie followed me.

Chuck slid a couple of ones across the counter towards Ben.

"No, keep it." Ben waved away the change and tucked his wallet back into his suit jacket. "I have a couple hold outs, but I expect by the end of the month—"

"You'll be out of luck," I told him as I plunked our sandwiches onto the counter. "My dad has a plan to get the money."

"Oh, does he now?" Ben faced me. His schmoozing expression was replaced with a curious one.

"Yep. So you can forget about your plot to take over Main Street. My dad will never let it happen."

"Plot?" Ben sighed, a worn (contrived if you asked me) type of sigh. I had a feeling I was about to hear a rehearsed speech. "Aileen, you may think of me as a bad guy, but I'm not. There's no hero here and no villain. That store isn't going to stay open forever, and I'm trying to do your family a favor. This town needs to be cleaned up, and in order to do that, there have to be certain casualties. I wish you could see how this benefits everyone." Yep, definitely rehearsed.

I folded my arms across my chest. "We need that store."

"Do you?" He sounded almost sad when he asked it, and I wondered if he thought he was being genuine. Whatever it was, I wasn't buying it.

"More than you'll ever know."

"Then I guess we'll agree to disagree." He tipped an imaginary hat, then focused his eyes on Jamie beside me. "Hey, you're that Flannigan kid, aren't you?"

"Yes," Jamie said slowly.

"It's a shame about your kin." It wasn't so much an expression of sympathy as it was a statement of fact.

Jamie narrowed his eyes. I would have too. His cousin had been murdered in cold blood, the town had been gossiping about it nonstop, and all Ben could do was call it a shame. "Uh, thanks."

"No problem. You take care now." He patted Jamie on the shoulder, cocked a finger gun at Chuck, and said, "Call me. We'll go fishing sometime."

"Will do."

As Ben strode out the door, I took deep breaths. How dare he suggest that he was helping us? Did he *want* us to lose our home? Maybe it was some kind of twisted payback for Mom dumping him. Well, he deserved it. And he'll deserve it even more when my dad forces him to eat his words.

"Aileen." Jamie put his hand on my shoulder. I shrugged it off.

"I'm fine."

"No, you're not. Who was that guy?"

As Ben climbed into his car, I stared laser beams at him, hoping he would spontaneously explode. "Ben Harwood. He keeps trying to buy my dad's store." In the cockiest voice I could manage, I said, "Let's clean up Main Street. Let's get rid of that smell. Puh. The only thing he's gonna get rid of is that stupid grin when he realizes Fish Tales isn't going anywhere."

Jamie laughed.

I put my hands on my hips. "I know you're not laughing at me."

"No, of course not." He straightened up, pretending to get serious, but instead of apologizing, he said, "You're cute when you're determined."

"I wasn't trying to be cute. I meant what I said."

"I know, and I have no doubt you're gonna get what you want. But for now, let's forget about him. Please." He nudged me with his elbow a couple of times until I was forced to crack a smile. "Please. Please. Please."

His little pokes tickled, and I danced away from the assault. "Okay, fine. He's forgotten."

Chuck scanned the items, and I reached into my pocket to pull out a couple of bills.

Jamie waved me away. "This is my treat. I asked you out, remember." He handed over two tens. "Besides I feel a little guilty making you come with me to take this stuff to my sister. I meant to go there first but I ran out of time."

"It's okay. I want to go." I'd spent a lot of time worrying about her, and I hoped that getting to see her would ease some of that worry. As the cashier handed Jamie back his change, I started loading our purchases into the canvas bag he'd brought. When I got to my 7up, I remembered something. Or rather, I didn't remember it. "Wait a second. How did you know this was my favorite? I don't think I ever told you."

"Didn't you?" And when he raised his eyebrows and laughed, my blood ran hot through my veins.

The seal. I'd told him everything about me, including how I felt about Jamie. I slammed the soda onto the counter and stormed out of the store. I was halfway across the parking lot when Jamie caught up with me.

"That's not fair," I said, whirling around to face him. "I didn't know that was you."

He reached for my hand, and I shoved it into my short's pocket. "Hey, don't be mad."

"That's easy for you to say. You didn't make a fool out of yourself in front of me." I'd told that seal how badly I wanted to kiss Jamie! More than once! In fact, I think I'd composed a soliloquy on it. And maybe a song. A few poems. Oh, he was gonna get it!

"I'm sorry. I didn't know how else to get you to talk to me." He tried to pry my hand free, but I wouldn't budge. In fact, I even stepped backwards. "Okay, fine. You want to get even?" He took a deep breath, the kind Dad always called courage builders, and said, "I'm afraid of snakes."

I narrowed my eyes. "What?"

"You want embarrassing? Here it is. When I was ten, Bridget and I were playing on the beach, and I swore I saw a rattlesnake."

"But they don't live on the coasts of Oregon."

"Try telling ten-year-old me that. Anyway, I ran screaming into my house, straight to my mom. A minute or two later, Bridget came in carrying a curvy, round stick. She handed it to me and said, 'I know. I would have been scared too. If I was three.'"

A smile cracked through my glare. How could I stay mad when there was teasing to do? "Oh, I don't know. Sounds pretty traumatic to me."

Jamie grimaced. "Sure, it sounds funny now. Back then, she spent days chasing me with that thing, leaving it in my bed, in the bathtub, under the couch cushions where I usually sat, and laughing hysterically, because I would freak out every time." While pouting adorably, he tugged my hand out of my pocket. This time I let him. "How's that?"

"Meh," I shrugged, stepping closer to him. I was still smiling, but I thought (hoped?) he caught what was beneath the smile. "I think I need more."

"Oh, really?" His voice turned from joking to deep and melodic. His gaze intensified with a look I'd only seen in the movies. Yeah, he caught it. He gave me a half-smile that edged its way inside of me, swirling and dipping into some very interesting places.

"Uh huh," I said, though I'd forgotten what we'd been talking about. Heck, I'd forgotten how to breathe.

"All right then. What about this?" He slipped his arms around my neck and dropped his voice to a whisper. "There's this girl I really like. I screwed things up with her, because I couldn't tell her something. I was miserable without her, so one day I waited for her after school to apologize, but when she showed up with her friend, I lost my nerve. Then she came to me, and she told me the one thing that made everything better. She knew my secret, and she still agreed to go out with me."

His whispers tickled my ear. I titled my head up toward him, bringing our faces so, so close to each other. Closer than they'd been on the beach. "You were really miserable without me?"

"I couldn't stay away."

The same pull I felt, the one that said we were meant to spend our days together. And as I relaxed into his arms, our future wrapped itself around us. My skin burned hot, though I was no longer embarrassed. This was something much deeper. As his lips brushed against mine, I closed my eyes and sank into him, forgetting about everything else. Jamie, his touch, his kiss, his breath, his arms, his sighs . . . those were the only things that mattered.

Eventually a car honking made us jump apart. Guess we'd both forgotten we'd been standing in the gas station parking lot. Jamie yelled out, "Sorry," and we took off, laughing and holding hands.

We made our way down the winding road out of town. It was only a mile or so, but we took our time, talking about nothing in particular and occasionally ducking into the forest on the side of the road to continue what we started in the parking lot. After a while, we turned down a dirt path that led deep into the woods. Before long, a tiny cabin came into view. It was nestled among some of the tallest trees, and I could hear the sound of crashing waves beyond it.

Huh. Neat place for a cabin.

Inside, it wasn't much—a kitchen/living room with a tiny hallway that led to a couple of rooms. At the end of the hallway was a screen door looking out over the ocean. There was no sound, except for the waves. The lights were off, and the surrounding trees made the room seem dark and a little creepy.

"Do you guys live here now?"

Jamie shrugged. "Temporarily. Though lately I guess all of our homes have been temporary to some extent. It's getting harder and harder to hide who we are, and we're having to move more often. Bridget hates it. Deirdre did too."

"And what about you?"

Jamie set the bag from the convenience store down on the counter and wrapped his arms around my waist. "Oh, I don't know. If we hadn't come back here, I never would have met you."

I slid my hands up to his chest and giggled. Just as I tilted my head up, a throat cleared in the hallway.

Jamie released me. "Hey, Dad."

"Hi, Mr. Flannigan," I said to the floor, certain my cheeks were as red as my t-shirt.

"Call me Liam, please."

"Okay." I nodded, not quite ready to say his name out loud. He was a parent, after all.

Clearly, Jamie wasn't as embarrassed as I was, because he acted like nothing had happened. Which it hadn't, technically. "How's Bridget?" he asked.

"The same, though she's been asking when you were gonna get back."

"Sorry. I, uh, got distracted." Jamie grabbed the bag and my hand and led me down the hall.

"I can see that," his dad called after us, and I could have sworn I heard a smile in his voice. Definitely not the reaction my mom would have had.

Bridget's room was just as gloomy and quiet as the rest of the house, but her face lit up when she saw us. "Hey, little brother." Her voice was rattly and weak, and her chest rose up and down in shallow puffs.

Jamie flicked on a bedside lamp, then laid the magazines beneath it on the table. "These are for you."

"Thanks. At least I'll have something to do while I'm awake now." From the looks of her, I hoped that wasn't very often. Her forehead glistened with sweat, but she also shivered. And those shivers caused her to wince. She didn't move to get the magazines either. I wondered exactly how much of her body was in pain. I had a feeling it was a lot more than she let on. "Can I ask you a favor?" There was none of the manipulation she had used the night of the bonfire. It was a simple request.

"Sure, Bridg," Jamie said, and with the somber way he spoke, I had a feeling he would have said yes to anything.

"Under my pillow."

Jamie reached under it, trying not to jostle her, and pulled out a folded slip of paper.

"It's for Kyle. Please get it to him. He works at the docks cleaning boats."

"I'm assuming Dad doesn't know about this."

"No, he'd kill me if he found out." She sounded so dejected, nothing like the spirited girl I first met. "Please. I just want to say goodbye. Dad took away my phone when he saw the texts."

"Goodbye? Don't talk like that. You'll get your skin back. You're not going to—"

"I know." She coughed and cried out with pain, as if emphasizing the exact opposite of what she was saying. Jamie sank down into the chair beside her. "But Dad and I had a long talk. He's right. Kyle is . . . different. He wouldn't understand about us." She looked to me, then back at Jamie. "You're lucky."

He took my hand and pulled me into his lap. "I know."

"Just think," she said. "Before long, I'll have my skin back, and Dad will be hauling us off to some other town. We won't even think about this anymore." She coughed again, and I wondered how much of her comment was truth and how much was her brave face. If I had to guess, I'd say about half and half. I didn't like those odds.

"Right." Jamie sounded just as enthusiastic as his sister, which is to say, not at all. I didn't think much of the idea either. She gets better and they move, or she doesn't get better. And they . . . what?

"Hey," I said. "Maybe when they find the hunter, you won't have to move. I mean, there won't be any reason to, right?"

Bridget smiled.

Jamie rested his chin on my shoulder. "I like that plan."

A few minutes later, Mr. Flannigan—Liam—came in carrying a lunch tray. My instinct was to jump out of Jamie's lap, but he held me firmly in place. The idea of anyone's parents seeing us cuddled up like that felt weird to me.

Liam set the tray down in front of Bridget. "What do you two have planned this afternoon?"

"Well, I kind of promised Aileen a picnic. Unless of course . . ." He looked to his sister.

"Go," Liam said. "I'll take care of her."

Bridget exchanged a look with her brother, like she might have said something different and changed her mind. But she worked up a smile anyway. "Yeah," she said, swirling her spoon in her soup. "Have fun. I'll probably take a nap after lunch anyway."

Jamie's father nodded, a firm line set to his lips. "Absolutely. You need your rest."

Bridget dropped her spoon and tucked her hands under the tray, her eyes cast down to her lap. Was she just tired, or was there something else?

Jamie must not have thought so, because he squeezed his sister's shoulder. "Okay, Bridg. We'll see you later."

Following his lead, I stood up and said, "Feel better."

We headed toward the door, but when we got to the hallway, Liam called Jamie back. "Can I talk to you for a second?" He gave me a look that said this was a family chat.

"Oh! Okay. I'll be," I hooked my thumb toward the back door, "outside."

"I'll be right there," Jamie said.

When I got out the door, I noticed an old pier jutting out into the water. I walked to the end of it, took off my shoes, and sat down.

It was a totally different view from the one I was used to. We were outside the bay, and while there were still rock islands popping up here and there, everything had a primitive, untamed quality. I liked it, and I could see why Jamie's family had chosen this spot. There was magic in the isolation.

The waves crashed around the pier, swallowing the pilings, then retreating, leaving me with a tiny sense of loss until they returned a moment later. A smile spread across my face. Something about the wildness made me want to jump in, but I knew that was a very, very bad idea.

"You like?" Jamie plopped down at my side and handed me my sandwich.

"Do you ever go swimming out here?"

"Don't even think about it," he said. "The current's a lot stronger here than it is in the bay."

"Got it." I pulled my feet up under me, so I wouldn't be tempted. But it was still there, calling to me. "Are you still willing to teach me to swim?"

"Sure. If you want."

"But it'd have to be at night. My mom, you know," I said, rolling my eyes.

"Oh, right, because of the accident."

"Unfortunately."

"I don't get it," he said. "You'd think she'd want you to learn after that. Have you tried talking to her about it?"

"She refuses to answer, and if I keep asking, she gets mad and makes me clean the kitchen." I still hadn't gotten over that summer when she made me mop the floor twelve times in one week.

"What about your grandmother? You said she helps sometimes."

I shook my head. "There are some miracles even Fee can't accomplish."

"But I can. We'll go swimming every night if you want."

"That'd be great." Talking about swimming and the accident triggered a question that had been bugging me for a while. "Hey, was it your family that rescued me back then?"

He smiled, like I had unlocked the door to a thousand year old secret. "There's always a few of us hanging around here."

"Really? Always?" I wondered how many of them were in my paintings, but decided I liked that mystery and wanted to leave that door locked for now. I'd have fun guessing later though. "Well, tell whoever it was I said thanks."

"No problem."

We ate in silence for a while, but when we were done and the crumbs had been fed to the fish, I asked Jamie, "So what did your dad want to talk about before?" It probably wasn't any of my business, but I was curious and thought he might tell me.

"Oh, that. Um, he wanted to let me know he might have a lead on the hunter. He's gonna go check it out tomorrow."

"He knows how to catch Mr. Glenn?"

"Yeah, I think so."

"Well, that's great! Everything's gonna be okay."

"I know. It's a huge relief." He stuffed our wrappers inside the bag and set it aside so he was free to put his arms around me and pull me close. "And with that off my shoulders, we're free to think about other things," he murmured into my ear. "I promised you the whole day and I haven't done a very good job of honoring that."

His nearness filled me up and made it difficult to think. "What did you have in mind?"

"Whatever." His lips touched my ear, and my hormones kicked into overdrive. "As long as it doesn't involve talking."

Kissing Jamie was exhausting. If I had known that, I would've probably taken a nap before he picked me up. Then I wouldn't have had the urge to take one after our long walk back from the cabin, because I absolutely, positively was not leaving his side until hell froze over, or until he dropped me off at my dad's shop, whichever came first. And even then, we had plans to meet for my first official swimming lesson after my parents had gone to bed.

As we reached the docks, I noticed how far the sun had traveled since we'd left my house. Far enough to make a long, bright streak across the ocean, one that blinded me if I looked straight at it, though it was still a few hours from setting.

Most of the boats were in for the night, and the only people hanging around were two college age boys scrubbing down Mont's boat. After Bridget had told me where Kyle worked, I knew who she was talking about. He and his friend had come into the store a little over a month ago, looking for work. I'd sent them down to the dock. Every summer we always had people passing through. Mr. Glenn would hire them on as handymen for a few months, and then they'd go on their way only to be replaced by new people the following year. Bridget had told us Kyle was tall and skinny with a rugged looking beard. I would have said the scruff looked more homeless than rugged, but that was just me.

Jamie and I dropped down onto the dock near Mont's boat, side-stepping to avoid the spray from Kyle's water hose. When he saw us, he gestured to his friend to cut the water.

Kyle dried his hand across the front of his torn white t-shirt and walked over. "Hey, what's up?"

"You Kyle?" Jamie asked.

"Yep." He didn't offer anything else, so Jamie continued.

"Um, you were dating my sister, Bridget?"

The other guy came up to us. He was stockier than Kyle with dark hair, and he reeked of cigarette smoke. "Bridget?" he said with a creepy guy smile. "That's that chick you were bang—"

"Robbie, shut it." Kyle elbowed him, hard. "This is her brother."

I held back a laugh. Jamie had a few inches on them both and could probably beat the snot out of them if he tried. And he looked like he might if Robbie finished that sentence.

"Oh, sorry," Robbie said, taking a step back. "No offense, dude."

"Sure." Jamie nodded, keeping his eyes locked on Robbie, glaring until the boy sniffed and looked away. Satisfied, his eyes flicked to Kyle. "Anyway, she wanted me to give you this." He pulled the note from his pocket.

Kyle glanced at it and smiled. "Awesome. Tell her I said thanks for *everything.*"

The insinuation was obvious in his words, and Jamie practically growled as they walked away. "I need to have a talk with my sister about her taste in men."

"Would she listen?" I replayed my mom's words from when we had talked about Jamie.

And I got the same answer. "Humph. Probably not."

I may not have understood Bridget's attraction to Kyle, but I knew what it felt like when you liked a guy, even if other people didn't think you should.

"Well, I should probably go meet my dad," I said reluctantly.

"Yeah. I'm gonna head back and try not to throttle my sister." He sounded just as unwilling as me, and as he closed the distance between us, my blood heated up once again. "I'll see you tonight?"

"You got it."

He gave me a kiss that threatened to pass the PG level, then headed off.

I sank down onto one of the huge, white dock coolers to wait until the dizziness wore off, and to watch him walk away. Just as I was about to get up, I heard a boat approach. It was Mr. Glenn's speedboat, and the person standing beside him had a beard that flashed red in the sun. Dad?

For a brief second, I wondered what he was doing on that boat. But then I remembered what Mr. Glenn was most likely doing.

I stared at my dad, but I could barely see him because of the horrible images taking over my mind. Bridget, Deirdre, both of them screaming, and Mr. Glenn and my dad . . . *No!* I closed my eyes and forced myself to think. There had to be some other explanation. My dad wouldn't do that, even if it meant losing our store.

As they pulled into the slip, I ducked down behind the cooler. My brain scrambled to come up with something reasonable. Maybe they were fishing. The catch was decent this time of year, and Mom didn't like him out on a boat, so he wouldn't tell her. That had to be it, right?

The motor quieted, and I peeked over the edge of the cooler.

Dad was leaning over the back railing securing one of the stern lines to the cleat on the dock. Mr. Glenn grabbed the spring line and carried it toward my dad so they could secure both ropes to the same cleat.

As the two of them worked, Mr. Glenn spoke to my dad. "We should try again tomorrow."

"I don't know. I hate to leave Mont alone at the store two days in a row. He likes to get some fishing in on the weekends."

Mr. Glenn lowered his voice. All I could understand were words like "bay" and "soon."

I shifted my feet under me and craned my neck up to hear better. One foot caught on a board that wasn't secure and slipped, causing a grating sound and a thunk as I fell to my knees.

Mr. Glenn stood up straight and looked around. There was no one on the dock but me, and I ducked behind the cooler. I didn't dare poke my head back up, but his voice still carried to me. "I'm paying you a lot of money to help me with this, Alex. Now I can ask someone else, but I'd prefer you do it. I know the water, but you know the islands and the caves. If anyone can help me find them, you can."

Dad sighed. I knew it was him, because it was the same sound he made whenever my mother won an argument. "Fine. Tomorrow then."

"Great." I could hear Mr. Glenn climbing onto the dock and stomping across it toward the stairs. "And, Alex? It's still hidden, right?"

"Yep. In the attic."

"Good. Make sure it stays that way."

# Chapter Fifteen

I ran all the way home, terrified of what I was gonna find in the attic, but unable to stop myself from looking.

Anything my dad hid in the attic would be with his old fishing junk. Mom hadn't wanted him to keep it, but he tucked it away up there and jokingly told anyone they'd lose a finger if they touched it. Mom let it be, knowing she had gotten what she wanted—a family stuck on dry land.

I sifted through Dad's old equipment, finding nothing but boxes of rubber bait, various sized hooks, dusty tackle boxes, and tangled fishing lines. Nothing that would be worth hiding.

*Where is it, Dad?* Although I refused to imagine what *it* could be.

I shoved aside more piles of junk and coughed through the billowing clouds of dust. I waved the filth away from my face and worked my way closer to the wall. The longer I searched, the more I scared I became. Whatever secret my dad had up here, he had buried it deep.

Fear kept making me want to stop, so I took my dad out of the equation and focused on Bridget lying broken in that cabin. I was doing this for her.

I edged myself between an overturned rowboat and a pile of bait buckets and stubbed my toe on a loose nail. Stars burst in front of my eyes.

*Dammit!*

I shook the tingles out of my foot and stepped on the nail with my sneaker, trying to push it back down. The nail didn't budge, but the other end of the board, half hidden under some fishing poles, popped up and then clunked back into place.

*Huh.*

I pushed my dad's equipment out of the way, grabbed the tiny stub of nail, and pulled. The entire board came out, all four feet of it. This far away from the light, it was hard to make out what was under the floorboard, but the dark and darker shadows told me there was definitely something. I moved some more of my dad's things and tugged on the surrounding boards, pulling out three in total. Then, I felt around in the hole with my hands. Something leathery and a little prickly lay inside. I yanked my hand out.

A sick knot formed in my stomach, confirming what I had suspected back at the docks, but still refused to believe.

My dad. The man who insisted on live traps whenever we got mice in our garage. The man who refused to let Mont hang his prize tuna near the bait cooler in the store even though it was good for advertisement. The man who sang to me to sleep every night until I was ten, because he knew those old sea songs brought me sweet dreams. Oh God, how could my dad be involved in this? My hands shook as I stuck them in again and pulled.

There was only one skin, and I held it up in front of me. It was nearly six feet long, with thick, tan fur and brown freckles. Whose was this—Bridget's or Deirdre's? And was the other one already gone? Sold? I clutched my stomach trying to hold back the nauseous rumbling down there. The floor swam before me. I fell to my knees.

"No no no no no!"

Then, "Daddy . . ."

The whisper shook my world. He couldn't possibly be involved. There had to be another explanation. And I had to hear it now. From him.

I tucked the skin in a faraway corner and scrambled down the ladder, not stopping to replace the ladder or even to lock the front door. I froze on my front porch though, my eyes darting across the yard.

My bike. Where the *hell* was my bike? Then I remembered I'd left it in the garage after school yesterday. Had that only been yesterday?

I peddled hard all the way to my dad's shop, stopping only when oncoming cars made me, and only then when the blare of their horns shocked me into reality. I didn't know what I was going to say to my dad, maybe beg him to tell me it wasn't true, maybe scream at him and threaten to call . . . who? Jamie's family didn't want the police involved, and I didn't know if I could do it anyway. He was my dad, for God's sake.

I dropped my bike in the alley behind Fish Tales and stormed in the front door. "Dad? Dad!"

"Calm yourself, little one. He ain't here." Mont stepped back from the bait cooler and shut the door, wiping his hands on his apron.

"Well, where is he? He hasn't come home yet."

"He stopped by an hour or so ago. Said he had some errands to run." He cocked his head, and the worn scar across his forehead twisted into a wrinkle. "Is something wrong?"

No, not something. That word implied a trivial idea, like I had a bad dream and I could chase away the monster by turning on the light. But this was no dream, and a thousand suns couldn't chase away this monster.

I peered out the front door down to the docks, drumming my fingers against the glass. No sign of him. Where had he gone? "Um, Mont, did my dad mention anything to you about where he was going today?"

Mont straightened up, well as straight as his years allowed, and frowned. "Ain't none of my business. Ain't none of yours either. I just know that whatever he's doing, he's bound and determined to save this store and keep your family in that nice little house of yours."

Any hope I'd been harboring that somehow he was innocent crashed through the floor. That look on Dad's face the last time I gave him money was etched in my memory. The pain. The desperation. My knees felt weak, or maybe the floor was about to give away. "He'd do just about anything, wouldn't he?"

Mont's face softened as he caught hold of my arm and led me back to the office where I could sit down. "He'd do anything for you."

"Yeah," I said, collapsing into the chair, hoping it would keep me from falling over. From falling apart. What was I supposed to do? Who was I supposed to go to? Then, I realized the perfect person might be standing right in front of me. "Hey, Mont. You know about selkies, right?"

The bell on the front door jingled. Instead of tending to the customer, Mont shut the office door, and moved closer to the table. I was glad for it. The customer could wait. This was more important.

"Some," he said softly. No reason for this conversation to carry into the store. "Why do you ask?"

I pressed my palms against my eyes, trying not to cry. I had to get the words out, because right then, Mont seemed like the only person I knew who could talk some sense into my dad. Who else would even believe me? "I think my dad's hunting them."

"Well, that's an interesting theory." Interesting. Not wrong. He didn't say it was wrong. "How do you figure?"

"A pelt," I whispered, the sound clawing its way through my throat. "There was a pelt in my attic."

He drew in a long, slow breath. The air whistled between his teeth. "I see." He watched me, the wrinkles around his eyes twisting in odd patterns until a crash just outside the office door caused us both to jump.

Mont flung open the door.

Kyle was bent over, picking up a tray of business cards he had knocked from the cash register stand. "Oh, hey there." Kyle cut his eyes over to me and saluted.

I didn't have the energy to respond, so he shrugged and turned back to Mont.

"I was just leaving you a note," he said. "We cleaned the boat and patched that gash in the hull. The left railing is rotten. We've ordered the part, but it may be a few weeks before it gets here."

"Great. Thanks."

"If you don't have anything else, we've got another boat to work on."

"No, you go on now," Mont said in a rush. "You've got plenty of customers at that dock to keep satisfied."

"A'right." He stuffed the cards back in their holder and headed out the door. "Peace."

Mont grumbled something about an idiot kid as he shut the door. "So, you think your Daddy's up to something."

I took his hands and squeezed them hard, pleading with him. "Can you talk to him, please? Tell him that . . . that we'll find another way. I'll give him every cent I earn. I'll live on store leftovers and expired food and won't complain. I'll do anything. He just can't do . . . *that.*"

He squeezed back, the calm in his face not exactly reassuring me, but at least settling me. For now. "I'll do what I can."

As I was leaving, I noticed another bright yellow flyer had been tacked to the center of our bulletin board. "Seal Bay Traders. Just what the fish ordered. Coming Soon."

How I wished that jerk had been the attacker instead of my dad.

I didn't remember riding home, but when I got there, I felt like I'd been drowned, resuscitated, and drowned again, a thousand times over. I could barely breathe, and the tears slicked my face like rain on a window. Fee was in the living room absorbed in the evening news, but even she couldn't make me feel better tonight. I passed her by without a word and locked myself in my room, curling up on my window seat, wishing I could shrivel into the tiniest ball ever. Then, maybe it wouldn't hurt so much.

Why had Dad thought this would make things better? Did he even know what he was doing? Maybe he didn't. The thought formed hopefully in my mind. Maybe Mr. Glenn had lied to him. As far as I knew he hadn't been involved with the actual attacks. Maybe my dad didn't realize they were hunting people. But that didn't change the fact he was illegally hunting seals. Fortunately my brain came up with an excuse for that too. Dad could have been told they were just looking for seals that were already dead. Ones that had been trapped in nets or died of natural causes. Still illegal, but not so terrible. That had to have been it.

Oh, please God, let that be it.

I tried calling Jamie. He didn't answer, so I left a message on his voice mail. Nothing elaborate. Just that he needed to call me, or come over, or . . . make it all go away. Yeah, that would be the best thing.

I stared out the window, wishing I could dive into the ocean and swim forever, until I reached another country. Another land. Another time.

Except I couldn't swim, so I stayed on my window seat wishing and hoping, until Fee knocked on my door.

"No, thank you," I said.

"Aileen, open up." Her voice pulsed with the cut-the-crap tone she usually reserved for my mom.

I slipped off the seat and shuffled across the room to unlock the door.

Instead of the anger I expected, she looked unsure. As unsure as I felt about everything. "Sit down, little pup," she said softly.

I retreated to my window seat where I pulled my legs up under my chin. With only a little effort, she lifted herself out of her wheelchair and joined me.

Watching me carefully, she said, "Are you going to talk to me, or do I have to pry it out of you?"

I shook my head, though I didn't know which question I was answering. Everything seemed jumbled up. Impossible to identify. Though there was one thought that stuck out above them all. "Dad," I squeaked.

"What about your father? Is something wrong? Is he hurt?"

"No. He's—" The words clumped together in my throat. I didn't know how to get them out. How was I supposed to face him after this? How could I face anything? But then Fee took my hands in hers. She felt strong and steady. She knew about selkies. She might be able to help. And honestly, I couldn't do this alone. Not anymore. "The Flannigans." The memory of Bridget lying on the beach flooded my mind, and I had to swallow back the pain. The next words, however, hurt even more. "Dad's hunting them. The selkies. I . . . I found—"

Fee gasped, but it wasn't surprise or horror or any of the million other reactions I'd expected. It was relief. Understanding. What in the world? "So that's what you found in the attic. I noticed the ladder was down when I got home. I should have known."

I couldn't speak. She knew? *She knew??* I yanked my hands away from hers. Maybe I should have gone out into the ocean, because I certainly didn't want to be here anymore. Even drowning would be better than this. A sharp pain cut through my chest, like I was already submerged, fighting for air.

I looked out my window, my eyes darting up and down the beach. I could still go. I could find Jamie and run . . .

"Stop, child." Fee grabbed my shoulders, and only then did I realize how badly I'd been trembling. Her expression stayed soft as she rubbed her thumbs across my knuckles and waited for my attention. It was something she'd done when I'd get upset as a child. It had always calmed me then. Just now, I didn't want to be calm, but I didn't know what else to do besides run. And with nowhere to go, I'd end up more lost than I was now.

I lifted my eyes to hers, wanting to be found.

"The selkies are in danger, yes, but your father's no more a threat to them than I am." She spoke slowly, each word a test to see if I was following her. She waited until I nodded, then she said the words that changed everything. "That skin in the attic? It's mine."

# Chapter Sixteen

"What?" Maybe not the most eloquent response, but it was all I had. Of course, after the most ridiculous day ever, I had a right to stupid questions. I'd started the afternoon with my first real kiss, which should have been monumental, but now it seemed so far away it was like it happened in another life. Then I spent hours thinking my father was a murderer, but didn't get to feel any relief when I found out he wasn't, because the reason he's innocent is because my grandmother is a freaking selkie! I mean, how much more was I expected to handle?

From the look on Fee's face, I had a feeling the answer was *A lot.* She took my chin firmly in her hand. "We need to talk."

"You go first, because I don't even know where to start."

"We start with Quinn Flannigan."

"Jamie's uncle?"

She nodded. I got the feeling that it wasn't an affirmation. She was preparing herself to finally tell the story. The one with the heartbreak.

Goose-bumps caught hold of my body, and I shivered, sensing the importance of it all. "What happened?"

"This isn't the first time the selkies in this area have been hunted. It happened when I was a child, and again when Quinn and I were dating. That time was the worst. We buried cousins, aunts, uncles, and grandparents. Quinn's mother, my sister, and ultimately even

Quinn." Fee's eyes grew moist in the corners. I pulled a tissue off my nightstand and handed it to her. She took it and squeezed my hand. "Thank you."

"So that's why you left. No wonder you couldn't handle that life anymore."

"It was more than that. I didn't *want* it without Quinn by my side. He was joyful and adventurous. He convinced me that we were invincible, but when he and Molly were both taken, I realized how fragile life really was."

"Molly?"

"My younger sister."

"Oh." She'd never mentioned one before, but it made sense. I even knew what she looked like. In Fee's photo album, there were half a dozen pictures of a little girl with long, black braids and Fee's commanding eyes. I'd always though she was a cousin. I'd never guessed how much more she was.

"Her death was the most brutal of all. Even your mother doesn't know the details." Fee's voice filled with cracks, and in between I could hear the tears struggling to break free. She held them back, though. The story came first. "I was eighteen at the time, but she was only nine. It was summertime. She was playing in the ocean when they took her. We were all there—my parents, Quinn, his father— but no one saw anything. Molly would go under for long periods of time. She liked to search for treasure on the ocean floor. She would find things too. One time, she surfaced with a gaudy emerald ring in her teeth. She wore that thing everywhere." Fee chuckled at the memory, but the laugh caught somewhere in her chest, and it choked her.

"Fee?"

She pressed the tissue to her mouth as she coughed out the broken words. "We . . . buried her . . . with that ring." I grabbed her hand between both of mine and tucked my head against her shoulder. I'd never seen her cry like this, and it truly scared me. She pressed her mouth to the top of my head, taking deep, shuddering breaths.

"Why don't you skip this part? It's too hard."

"No," she said. "You need to know everything."

If it was all like this, I wasn't sure if I wanted to. But maybe it wasn't so much that I needed to hear it. Maybe she just needed to tell it.

After she gained control of the tears, she continued. "Later, we found out the men who caught her had been scuba diving in our waters for weeks. They knew who we were, and they weren't going to stop until they had all of us, starting with the smallest and the weakest. Molly surfaced further down the beach and went into a little cave where she kept her collection. She changed into human form, and you can guess who followed her there and what they did to her."

I didn't want to guess, but the sight of Bridget and the sound of her jagged breathing, flooded my mind.

Fee's mind was full too. Her eyes glazed over as she relived the horror of that day. "We found her in that cave, beaten, lifeless. They'd even stolen her treasures, everything but the ring which we found clutched in her hand."

"Oh my God." Now I definitely didn't want to hear any more of this. The nausea from earlier returned in full force. I drew my knees up under my chin and tucked my head between them. I took deep, gulping breaths, desperate for the aching and churning to stop, but afraid that it never would. I had heard the words, imagined the scene. Those things couldn't be undone no matter how hard I wished.

Fee's hand came to rest on my back. "I know, baby. Believe me, I know."

"So, the people responsible were never caught?" I asked with my forehead pressed against my knees.

"No, they were," she said. "There was a team. Their leader was Michael Glenn."

"Who's that?" Of course the last name was familiar to me, but I couldn't place the first.

"Your friend Ian's great uncle."

Now I sat up. "What happened to him?"

Fee understood why I'd asked that question and shook her head. "It's not him this time. He died in jail a few years back. His brother, Ian's grandfather, made sure he was jailed for murder. He had just graduated law school and had little tolerance for anyone who broke the law. I owe him my life. All of the selkies do."

"Did he know you were selkies?"

"There are a few humans who know. He was among them."

"Well, how can you be sure Ian's dad is on your side? His father may have helped you, but his uncle was hunting you."

"I've known Isaac Glenn since the day he was born, and he has never been anything less than honorable. And if your dad is working with him, well that should be proof enough Isaac is on our side."

I suddenly felt ashamed I had ever doubted my father. My instinct had told me I was wrong. I should have listened, but how was I supposed to know where the skin had come from? And if neither one of them was guilty, I was back to square one. My theory about the toothless, tattooed guy seemed likely once again. I wondered what Mr. Glenn's uncle had looked like. "So, after Quinn's death, you gave up being a selkie and moved to Ireland."

She nodded. "It was hard, willingly separating myself from that life, but in the end I knew it was the right choice for me. I needed to be with humans. One human in particular."

"Grandpa Colm."

"I presented him with my skin so he would know that I'd never leave him. He didn't need the promise, but I needed to give it. It was both the easiest and the hardest thing I've ever done."

"Why?"

"If someone takes the skin from you, the pain is excruciating. The heartache can break you down, change you. After all, you're being cut off from a part of your soul."

I thought of how Bridget had changed from the time I met her until the time I saw her in the cabin. She had lost so much of her will. She had given up. Even if you survived, that was no life for anyone. "Is giving it away any different?"

"If you willingly shed your skin and present it to someone you love, it's not so bad." She did a double blink to erase tears, memories, whatever. Then she smiled. "With the right person, the pain fades with time. Their love fills in the gaps. It heals you."

"But he's gone now. The skin is yours again. Does that mean you could slip into it and go swimming?"

"It doesn't work like that. Once you willingly give it up, it's gone. The magic won't work for me anymore."

"Would you go back to it if you could?"

She smiled a secret little smile, and I guessed the answer was yes, no matter what she said. "I still have the ocean. Nothing can take that away from me."

I knew the feeling. I walked over to my desk and picked up a photo of me and my parents. I was maybe two, and we were standing on the deck of dad's old boat. "So Mom and Dad know about this?"

"They know enough." Fee pushed herself up and came to stand behind me. She rested her hands on my shoulders and squeezed them, both for her own support and for my reassurance. "Your father adores the selkies. He would never, ever do anything to hurt them. You have to understand that."

I traced my thumb over my mom's face. I could tell from her frustrated expression that she was trying to get me to face the camera, but my gaze was fixed on the water. "And Mom?"

"She's a different story. Your mother is afraid of the selkies, of what they can do." Fee paused to make sure I was listening.

I kept very still to show her that I was.

"She doesn't want them to take you away."

I set the picture down and faced her. "Okay, now I'm really confused."

"I may have given up my life with them, but the choice still lies with my child. Full blooded selkies are born as seals with the ability to transform into a human. Selkies who give up their skin give birth to human children, but those children have the right to inherit their parent's skin. Your mother could have taken my skin, along with all of the joy and freedom ... and danger that goes with it."

"But she didn't."

"Ultimately, no." Fee made her way back to the seat and sat down, angling herself so she could see out the window. She pressed her fingers to the glass, touching the horizon.

I had that habit too, whenever the land felt like it was closing in on me.

"She's a different person than us. She denies the call of the ocean, but as you've probably noticed, she can't distance herself from it either. For a while she accepted your father's job as a fisherman, but after the accident, she let fear take over. She became convinced the accident was the selkies' fault. Since they couldn't have her, they would take you."

I tried to remember what had happened that day, and in the days that followed, but the memories were nothing but faded watercolors. Blurry lines that hid the truth. "Did they?"

She turned back to me. Her love of the selkies warmed her expression. "No, child. They protected you. They kept you safe until I came to retrieve you."

"So you're saying she was a selkie until the accident?"

"No. There are other reasons she chose to remain human, but they would be best coming from your mother."

I humphed. "Like she would ever tell me anything."

"You're getting older, and you're closer to the ocean than she ever was. It scares her. But I think some part of her also understands. Give her a chance, little pup. She may surprise you. Besides," her cheeks puffed into a soft, round smile, "I can't act as your buffer forever, now can I?"

I really wished she could. Fee overestimated my mom sometimes. "Does this mean what I think it means?"

She leaned forward and lowered her voice. "Your mom has one secret she kept from you, one I feel it's time you learned." Her eyes grew huge and intense, filled with a message I was slowly beginning to understand. "She doesn't want you to know who you really are."

*The choice still lies with my child.* For most of my life I'd thought it was just a love of the water, then when Jamie appeared, I figured it must have been him. Thinking back, I suppose I'd always known it was more than that. But how much more, I had never imagined. "I'm a selkie." The words felt strange, raw and perfect.

"By all rights, the skin now belongs to you. Tell me, what do you feel when you're standing by the ocean? What do you feel when you trail your fingers through the water?"

Honestly? "Magic."

Fee smiled. She knew my answer before I said it.

I crossed back to the seat and perched next to her, my mind full of twisting emotions: how, and when, and what the hell, and yes, *yes*, YES!

"So what do I do now?"

Fee took a hunk of my hair and smoothed it away from my face. It felt like she was trying to brush away my worries and send them into the wind. "The choice is up to you."

# Chapter Seventeen

I sat in the darkest, emptiest corner of the attic, the side of my head pressed against the angled roof. If I moved, splinters snagged my hair and scratched my head, so I kept still and listened to the creaks of the house settling around me. The seal skin, *my* seal skin, lay across my lap. Its heaviness pinned me to the floor.

Numbness. Comfort. Fear. Excitement. Confusion. Each emotion raced inside of me, refusing to be harnessed. Yet underneath them all, strong and just as untamable, ran an undercurrent of certainty. This was what my life had been missing all along. I belonged in the ocean. It would be easier to remove one of my fingers than it would to get me away from the water. I could be a selkie, something my body had been reaching for my entire life.

A selkie.

Who couldn't swim.

How was I supposed to get around that?

I stretched my legs out in front of me and breathed through the hours. For a while, a few slants of light peeked between the rafters, but they muted and eventually went away altogether.

Sometime later, the ladder dropped out of the floor, shooting a rectangle of light up to the ceiling. I blinked at the sudden intrusion, but didn't respond.

Mom's head poked through the hole. "Hey, got some time to talk?"

I shrugged. It didn't matter what I said, she was climbing up anyway. And though I wouldn't admit it to her, I sort of wanted her to. Fee had answered a lot, but there was still so much I didn't know. Hell, I felt like I knew nothing.

She popped the string on the light bulb. It swung back and forth, and as she picked her way around our belongings, the light threw long mom-shaped shadows all over the walls. I patted the floor next to me as she approached.

She pulled the blanket off my Little Tykes kitchen set and spread it out so she could sit on it. I didn't mention there was probably more dust on the blanket than on the floor. That would have earned me a glare I didn't care to see right now.

With her hands clasped in her lap, she stared at the opposite wall, just like me. "So," she said.

I ran my palms along the length of the pelt. "Yeah."

She had left the hatch open, and I could hear the TV going downstairs . . . some detective show Fee watched. While Mom pretended she couldn't see what was in my lap, I tried to figure out which episode Fee was watching. It took exactly five seconds to decide I didn't care.

"Why didn't you—" I began, just as she said, "Your grandmother shouldn't have told you."

Really? She came to tell me *that?* Anger boiled in my chest, setting fire to my words. "No, *you* should have. A long time ago. How could you keep something like this from me?"

"I was protecting you, Aileen. You didn't need to know this. You never needed to know."

"I *always* needed to know!"

My voice had gotten so loud that Dad called up through the hatch, "You two okay up there?"

"Fine, Dad." I took a deep breath and when I spoke to my mom again, I lowered my voice, but not the intensity. "God, Mom, don't you know me at all? How often have I asked you to teach me to swim? How many hours do I spend staring out at the ocean, drawing it, memorizing it, wanting to be a part of it?"

"Too many."

"Why is it too many? What's so wrong about being who I am?"

"It's not who you are. It's who *they* are."

*You mean the hunters?* I almost spit it out, but then clamped my mouth shut. She may have known about Fee's past, but she didn't know what was going on now. At least I didn't think so. I buried my hands in the fur to give them something do, to keep from clenching them in fury. She already made her decision. Why couldn't she let me make mine?

"I've never told you how I met your father."

*What?* I turned to see her looking straight at me, the anger suddenly gone, replaced with a softness she usually reserved for Dad alone. "I thought you two met in college."

"No," she said. "We didn't." Mom kept so much locked inside of her. Some days, I could almost see the tense little balls of stress knotted inside her muscles. But now, for the first time, she was about to let something out. To me! It startled me, but it calmed me too, eased me in to what she was saying. She sighed as she pulled one end of the pelt over her lap, touching it gently like a long lost friend. "I was eighteen, and I was so much like you."

"How?" It wasn't a challenge, just a question. I couldn't imagine my mom ever needing to beg for swimming lessons, or wondering why she felt like she belonged in the water. Then again, Fee probably hadn't kept secrets like that.

"I was young." Mom looked away, hiding her face in the shadow, though she couldn't hide her sniffle. "I didn't listen to my mom's warnings, and I swam out past the bay one afternoon, alone."

"As a seal?"

"Yes," she said solemnly. "I didn't have any friends to swim with. In fact, the only other selkies Fee had introduced me to spent most of their time as seals. I never wanted that type of life, but I did love to swim, to explore the reefs, to search deep and far, to have no boundaries . . ." A swallow went down her throat. ". . . to see what was out there."

"And what did you find?" I whispered, afraid of the answer, but thrilled that Mom had once understood the need to explore.

She focused back on me, her eyes glistening in the dim light. "A net."

I clutched the pelt even harder. "They were hunting you?"

"No," she said firmly. "They were fishing, but I got caught in the net."

"Did they know you were a selkie?"

She shook her head, though whether it was to answer me or to chase the fear away, I couldn't tell. Maybe it was both. She took my hand. Another first. "They didn't know I was there until I had almost drowned. I was hopelessly tangled in the net; I couldn't surface to breathe. By the time your father finally raised the net—"

"Wait, Dad?"

Mom pinched her eyes shut, and a single tear drop rolled down her cheek. "By the time he pulled me up, I was nearly gone. Somehow, he got me breathing again. And just before he released me, he knelt down, looked into my eyes, and said, 'You're gonna be okay. I'll watch out for you from now on. I promise.' "

I pinched the bridge of my nose, holding back my own tears. I could picture it all, Mom looking up into Dad's eyes, the sun a halo around his strawberry blonde hair. "And did he?"

She nodded. "When he pulled into the dock, I was there waiting for him with a very interesting story."

"And he believed you." I supplied the ending myself, knowing every word was true. Of course my dad believed her. He would have never thought otherwise. "Did you give up your selkie for him?"

"I did. Because that day I realized no matter what you do, there's always something. The hunters that got Fee's sister. Fishermen with their nets. Sharks." A small laugh on the last word told me there was another story there. For another day. Today, we needed to finish this talk.

"But Mom, there's always something, whether you're a selkie or a human, or a cat curled up on a porch. Fee says that trouble will find you no matter where you are, if it's looking hard enough."

"I know, sweetie." She slipped her arm around my shoulder and pulled me to her. "You really are just like me. Stubborn as all get out."

I tilted my eyes up toward her. "So what are you saying?"

She took a loud breath and puffed out her cheeks. "Fee told me about the Flannigans. If you want to spend time with them, the decision is up to you, but you know what I think you should choose."

I wanted to ask if she had ever regretted her decision, but I realized I already knew the answer. That night I'd seen her crying out on our pier . . . she hadn't been crying for Grandpa Colm. She'd been crying for the life she left behind. And now she was passing that life, and all of its wonders, to me. "So you're . . . you're saying yes?"

"I'm saying you wouldn't listen to me if I said no, and I don't have the patience for you sneaking around behind my back." And with that, the wistful, sharing Mom was gone, replaced with sharp edges and strict lines. But there was one place, right above her eyes, that didn't seem as hard anymore. Was that where she had kept the secret?

"Thank you. For talking to me." I couldn't believe I'd actually won.

She patted my shoulder once before getting up and brushing the dust off her pants. "Dinner's in the fridge. Don't wait too long, okay?"

"I won't," I promised as she descended through the hole in the floor. I'd waited long enough.

# Chapter Eighteen

Early Sunday morning, Jamie showed up at my back door wearing his swimsuit. After I had come down from the attic, I saw he'd finally called back, though he hadn't said much in his voice mail. I sent him back a simple text.

*I know the family secret. Will you teach me how it works?*

The answer came back quickly, as if he knew. As if he'd been expecting me to ask all along.

*Tomorrow. 6 am.*

So at 6:01, Jamie took my hand and led me down the porch steps into the sand. I slung my backpack over my shoulder, heavy with the weight of my pelt.

*My* pelt. Would I ever get used to that?

We made our way down the beach toward a small cave at the edge of the water. I couldn't walk slowly; each step was practically a skip. But Jamie's turtle pace and solemn expression kept me reined in.

"What's wrong?" I asked. My pack bounced against my shoulder blades as I danced a little jig in front of him. "Do you need some of my mom's coffee? I'm sure she's brewing a pot by now."

A hiss of laughter escaped his lips. "Nah, I'm good. But it looks like you've already had about twelve cups."

"Nope," I said. "This is pure adrenaline. Do you know how long I've waited for this? Well, not this exactly, because I didn't know all the details. I mean, who on earth would ever believe what's happening here. It's incredible. Don't you think it's incredible?"

Jamie's whole body shook in a gut-busting laugh, one that woke him up, brought him to life. With the laughter, his eyes took on a glow, the same look he had the first time he tried to kiss me. I had the sense to stop babbling as he took a step closer.

"Yeah," he said softly. He touched his hand to my face, and I felt the heat rush into my cheeks. It didn't stop the adrenaline, but it halted my bouncing. "It's pretty incredible."

I sucked my bottom lip into my mouth, then thought better of it. How was he supposed to kiss me if I was hiding half of my lips? It turned out to not be a problem. My body took over as he drew closer, two magnets coming together.

His kisses were so much deeper than they had been . . . yesterday? Had it only been yesterday? Wow, a lot had happened since then.

He pulled me tighter against him, a move that told me he never wanted to let me go. While he cupped my cheek with one hand, he snaked the other one around my waist, beneath the backpack. That action was our undoing, because the slight adjustment of the pack reminded me what I was here to do. And unfortunately, it wasn't to make out with Jamie. Not yet, anyway.

I pulled back an inch. Less than one. My lips trembled, wondering why I stopped. I put my hands on his chest to keep from falling back into him. "Um . . . later. Teach me to swim first."

He brushed his thumb across my cheekbone. His half smile tempted me to forget about the selkie lessons. And if that wasn't enough, he had to ask, "Are you sure?"

In answer, I backed up two giant steps, just out of his reach. Before he could protest, I gave him a wicked half smile of my own and started walking toward the cave.

He went directly to the back of the cave. The early morning sun didn't quite reach back there, but I could still see him crouched in the gray and black shadows, moving a pile of seemingly random rocks. When he was done, I noticed the rocks had covered a hole that ran underneath the back wall of the cave. He stuck his arm in up to his bicep and pulled out a black, cloth sack, roughly the size of my backpack. No need to ask what that was.

"Do you always keep that here?"

He shrugged. "I use a few different caves. Some on the beach, others out on some of the islands. I'm a pretty strong swimmer so I just swim back here as a human."

That's why he was always in his swimsuit. I didn't have one, so I'd just worn shorts and a tank top, hoping that'd be suitable. But what if it wasn't? A shot of panic rushed through me, prickling the hairs on my arm. "Wait a minute. Do I have to be . . ." I tugged on the hem of my shirt, unable to say the word naked in front of him. "Do I need to take my . . . um, my . . ."

He waggled his eyebrows and laughed, apparently enjoying my embarrassment.

"Stop it." I chucked a small rock at his feet.

He tried to snag it out of the air, but lost his balance and dropped down on his rear end. He tipped onto his back, his legs flying in the air, looking very much like a fish on the beach, flopping its way back to the water. I couldn't help laughing as he pushed his way back into a sitting position. Of course that was his cue to pick up the rock I had thrown at him and return fire. I caught it easily and stuck out my tongue, bringing my hand behind my head and aiming again. He threw his hands up in surrender. "Okay, fine. You win."

I dropped the rock and responded with a proud smile.

"In answer to your question," he said, swiping a hand through his hair and trying to restore some of his dignity, "you'll be fine. When you transform, it's like your mind is there, but your body is stored somewhere else."

"So when we're done, we don't pop out all slimy and gross?"

He made a face that looked both silly and scary in the long shadows, lots of strange angles. "What movies have you been watching?"

"None." I sat on the ground and pulled my knees up to my chin. "I just wanted to know what I was getting into."

He set his bag on the ground and settled in next to me. "Yeah, about that. Do you know what you're getting into? I mean, you know about the attacks. Maybe this isn't the best time to do this."

So that's why he hadn't been as excited as me this morning. Had he kissed me to try to stall me? What a bum. "Look, I know what's going on, but I'll be with you, right? They've only attacked people by themselves."

"So far, but—"

"Jamie." I put my hands on his and scooted around so I was facing him. "I need to do this. We could wait, but I wonder will there ever be a right time? A better time? The attacks have happened before and they will happen again. It doesn't change who I am." I pulled the pelt out of my backpack and spread it across my lap, my hands clutching it like a lifeline. "This is me. I've felt it my entire life, in every inch of my body, and I'm finally starting to understand it. I can't put my life on hold for fear that something might happen. I'm not my mom."

He placed his hands over mine, and as the sun poked its head into the cave, Jamie's face lit up with a brilliant fire. Although I suspected that light had little to do with the sun, and everything to do with the passion that burned inside him. The same one inside of me. "Do you promise to stay by my side every moment we're out there?"

"I promise." Hope fluttered in my chest, making me giggly and excited again. I was actually going to do this. I was a selkie. I was going to swim in the ocean and . . . wait. "I can't swim."

Jamie pulled his pelt out of the bag and laid it across his lap just like me. "That's not a problem either. Once you transform, it's all instinct. Seals can swim from day one. So can you." He pointed his finger at me, a warning in his voice. "But don't go jumping into deep water as a human. It doesn't work like that. The seal may know how to swim, but Aileen still doesn't."

"Got it," I said as I picked up my pelt and draped it over my shoulders like a cloak. Nothing happened, but I hadn't really expected it to. I brought the tail around to my face to examine it. The fan shaped flipper seemed so small and fragile. I wondered how much power it had. "So what do I do?"

"This." Jamie laid his pelt on the ground, the belly of it face up.

He looked at me and I copied him, laying mine out right beside his. They both had slits about three feet long running the length of them. He spread the slits open.

"Now what?" I asked.

"There's no real secret. If the magic is in you, it does most of the work."

I held the edges of the slit, unsure of what to do. Was this going to hurt? I hadn't thought about that before. "So I just climb in?"

"Feet first," he said, motioning for me to go ahead.

"Okaaaay." I slid my feet in towards the flippers. I thought it would feel strange, but really it just felt like I was slipping into a pair of footie pajamas, soft and comfy. I looked to Jamie once more, and he nodded.

"Go ahead."

I slid my legs all the way in and lay down. Before my back touched the ground, I felt something envelop me—a hot, tingly sensation that ran from the tips of my toes to the ends of my hair. It was like when I put my hands on that lightning ball at the science museum. Before long, my vision blurred out, and everything got too bright. I closed my eyes against the harshness. For a while I concentrated on my other senses, how my hearing had grown clearer, how my body didn't feel like my own, but didn't feel wrong either. Still me, but stronger, wilder.

When I finally opened my eyes, everything had shifted to gray-scale. I rolled over onto my stomach and noticed the sleek, dark

Jamie seal watching me. He blinked once, then angled his head toward the water as if to say, "You ready?"

I was one step ahead of him. I pressed my front flippers into the sand and pushed off, caterpillar crawling my way to the edge of the water. It wasn't far, maybe two feet from the mouth of the cave. I wiggled out into deeper water, looked back once to make sure Jamie was following, then ducked beneath the waves.

I took off, rocketing through the water at a speed I'd never be able to achieve while running on land. I dove deep, deep down, feeling the press of the water grow tight around me like a warm coat in winter, protecting me, welcoming me. Every muscle in my body worked separately and together, propelling me wherever I wanted to go.

I reached the sandy bottom and skimmed up and down along the valleys and hills. The seaweed tickled my belly, and the detail in the sand took my breath away. Each grain was a brilliant diamond, glittering with facets not visible through my human eyes, but stunning through the seal's vision.

I stopped for a while to scan the bottom for sea glass and heard a clicking sound next to me. *What's that?* I whipped my head to the right, my muscles rigid with panic. A diver? A shark?

Something nudged me. I started before I realized it was Jamie, directing me to the source—a crab scooting off to somewhere important. My body sagged with relief. Stupid crab. Why did it have to be so loud?

Jamie tilted his head as if to say, *You'll get used to it.*

And he was right. When I really focused on my hearing, I noticed how different everything sounded—amplified, with sharp as glass edges. I flicked my gaze around as I tried to identify every sound in the area. I heard the breaths of fish, the swishing of anemone, the song of the whales. I heard the sounds of distant seals calling to each other. I wondered where they were and if they wanted to join us. I looked back at Jamie, but he shook his head in a distinct "no" gesture and swam in the opposite direction. Ah, well. Maybe next time.

I followed him back to a series of underwater caves. After he passed by one, I ducked in, waiting to see if he noticed my disappearance. If we had been on land, he probably would have found me due to my sheer inability to hold back the giggles. As a seal, I remained quiet as a whisper. One second ticked by, two, and then his face appeared around the corner. Just as he registered my presence, I rocketed past him, ducking behind a nearby rock and baiting him to follow me.

Our game of cat and mouse was on.

We played for hours, diving under natural rock bridges, through tunnels, and in and out of caves. Jamie never let me get far, and I didn't really try. Half the fun was doing this with him. The other half was that stunned feeling I got deep down in my bones when I realized this was all real. I hadn't known the ocean contained such beauty before. I mean, I had seen pictures, but absolutely nothing could compare with living it, knowing I belonged to it.

Eventually, I swam up to the surface, exhausted and happy. Jamie popped up next to me, and the two of us floated on our backs, resting as the day grew brighter.

I never wanted to go in. If it hadn't been for school and family and all of that pesky stuff that gets in the way of fun, I might never have. The hours could turn into days and weeks and years, and with Jamie by my side, my life would be a perfect dream.

But even dreams must come to an end. Later that afternoon, we swam back to the cave where we shed our skins. It turned out to be as simple as taking a deep breath and imagining ourselves human again. The skin split open just like a zipper on a coat. It made me a little sad to separate myself from it, but I knew it was only temporary.

Jamie tucked his skin back in the hole, and I put mine back in my backpack. I'd have to think up a good hiding spot for it later.

As we were walking back to my house, I asked Jamie, "Can we do this again tomorrow? After school? Or maybe after dinner? Or both?" I imagined a lifetime of days like this, Jamie and I swimming, playing, and just being together. I'd finish school, and we'd travel the different coastlines, maybe even make it to Ireland one day. I could sell paintings in the little tourist towns, and he would fish.

"Um, I can't." And there was that look from this morning, that serious pouty look.

"Why not?" I asked. And yes, I pouted a little too. I may have hidden from him a couple of times today as a game, but I would never think of going into the water without him.

Jamie glanced over his shoulder toward his house. It looked dark and empty as usual. "You know how I said we move around a lot?"

I nodded.

"Well, my dad doesn't think we should stick around anymore. Not all of us. That's why I didn't answer right away last night. I was helping pack our things."

I stopped dead in my tracks. The idea of Ireland vanished into smoke. My back porch, maybe ten feet away, became a blur. "What?"

Jamie moved in front of me. He placed his hand under my chin, forcing me to look at him. It was hard, considering the tears that were surfacing. "We're moving. You should be safe here. Just hide your skin and—"

"Stop," I begged. The tears burst free, staining my cheek. I didn't have the energy to brush them away.

"Please, don't." He touched one of the tears with his thumb. It didn't help. They just came faster. "Dad and a couple of the others stayed behind to take care of something, and I asked to stay too. I . . . I wanted to tell you in person."

"How long?"

"I'll find a way to stay in touch with you. We'll be somewhere on the coast. We can still go swimming."

"How *long?*"

His eyes lifted from mine and glossed over as he gazed toward the horizon. "Tonight."

I pushed past him and ran up the steps to my house.

"Aileen, wait."

I heard his footsteps pounding behind me, but I didn't look back. I yanked open our back door and ran into the house. Mom and Dad would both be at work until later, but I wasn't looking for them.

"Fee!" I called. "Fee, where are you?"

I rushed into the living room where I could hear some commercial blaring on the TV. "Hey, why didn't you—"

Fee lay sprawled out on the oval rug, her legs cocked at weird angles, her head asleep in a pool of her own blood.

# Chapter Nineteen

I dropped my bag and screamed.

Jamie came running up to my side. "What? What is it?"

I didn't have to answer, though. He saw.

"Oh my God!" He dropped down by her head, touched her neck, felt her chest, all the things people do when they can't believe what's in front of them. His features fell as each test confirmed what I already knew. I couldn't feel her inside me anymore. She was gone.

I stood frozen in the doorway, doing nothing but wishing to go back in time to where I could stop this. Fix what was wrong. Erase that massive amount of blood matted into her beautiful gray braid. Heal those black, finger-shaped bruises on her arms. Remove the look of horror and betrayal from her face.

Jamie kept fussing over her until I said, "Don't."

"But we need to—"

"Stop it," I said with steel in my words. "Just close her eyes." Then he knew too.

With a shaky hand, he gently slid down her eyelids. And when that was done, he stood up, flung my backpack around one arm and grabbed me with the other. "Let's go."

I planted my feet. I hadn't moved since getting to the room. I wasn't gonna move now. Maybe never again. "No. We can't. My parents. The police. We need to do something."

"We *are* doing something," he insisted. "We're getting you out of here."

I yanked my arm out of his grasp. "I can't leave her!"

"Aileen, listen to me!" He grabbed me by the shoulders and forced me to look at him. "Whoever did this knew she was a selkie, and they'll know about you too. Since they obviously didn't find her skin," he nodded toward the backpack at my feet, "they're going to come back. What if they're still nearby? You're not safe here!"

I could hear the fear in his voice, hear what he was telling me, but it took a moment for it to sink in. I couldn't shake the feeling we had to do something for Fee. We couldn't just leave her there. It hurt my soul to even think it. "But what about . . ." My voice broke on her name.

Jamie took a long look at her. His eyes shone with dampness, and even though he hadn't known her, I could feel his heart breaking as much as mine. Or maybe I imagined it, because to me, the entire world was broken.

He tore his gaze away from her. "I'll call someone as soon as we get you out of here. But please, I need you to be safe."

I sucked my bottom lip in between my teeth and bit down hard. If walking in and finding her like *that* was horrific, walking away from her was a billion times worse. But Jamie was right. Since the hunters hadn't found the skin, they'd come back. Or maybe they were still close, watching for someone to come home. Through the living room window, I could see the empty street in front of our house and the tall pines that blanketed the other side of the road. Anyone could be there, waiting.

My feet moved backward on their own. My hand sought Jamie's and held on tight. His strong grip kept me grounded, not enough to make things better, but enough to keep me moving.

With one agonizing look at my grandmother, my confidante, my hero, I stumbled out the door.

Jamie and I ran down the beach to his pier where their rowboat was tied to one of the pilings. I climbed in, and he tossed me my backpack as I settled down on one of the two wooden plank seats. He untied the boat and jumped in after me. Before taking up the oars, he paused for a second. His shoulders sagged, and his whole face crinkled with a frown.

"You okay?" he asked.

"No." I didn't elaborate. Why should I? Instead, I clutched my bag tightly against my chest and stared out at the horizon. For all the good it would do me. Things weren't going to be okay for a very long time. The sight of . . . had opened up a giant gaping hole in my chest. Not even the ocean could fix that.

We rode in silence for a while, watching some storm clouds pile up in the distance, cutting off the sun. I hadn't asked where we were going. If he wanted to sail me over the edge, I would've been fine with that. But I guess he felt the need to tell me.

"There's an island about a quarter mile out, just past that larger one over there." He pointed to one of the big rock islands that peppered the water, one of a dozen I could see. When I was little, I always wanted to swim out and explore the islands. Now, I didn't give a flying flip about them.

"The cave is well hidden," he continued. "I don't think anyone knows about it outside of my family."

"It's fine," I mumbled. "Just get me there and get back to my . . ." God, I couldn't even say it. A flood of tears cut through my words. I had been holding back, numbing myself since The Moment. It wasn't working anymore. That empty hole inside of me opened its jaws and howled.

Jamie got me to the island, pulled the boat up on land, and steered me through a thicket of scrub that made my arms and legs bleed. I held tightly to my bag. It was my lifeline, my tie to her, my legacy.

Eventually, we found our way into a little cave with enough room for two or three people to lay side by side. I could stand up in it, but Jamie couldn't, so the two of us sat on the ground. I balled my bag up in my lap.

"What now?" I asked.

"I'm going back, telling my dad, getting some help."

"And then?"

"I'll come back as soon as it's safe. I'm leaving the boat here just in case you have an emergency. I can swim back."

"Are you sure?" He hadn't brought his skin with him. It would be just him, and it was pretty far.

He nodded. "I've done it tons of times. I'm more worried about you." His hand moved toward my bag. A section of the zipper had come undone, and he ran his fingers across the small section of my pelt that stuck out. "I don't have to tell you it's not safe to change, right?"

My mind flashed again to The Moment. I wanted more than anything to remove that image from my mind, but unless someone gave me a good, hard clunk on the head, it was there to stay. "Nothing's safe."

"Don't think like that. We're gonna stop this. There's only so many people who knew about your grandmother, right?"

"Right. My mom and my dad. Your family. Mr Glenn." I had been ticking the people off on my fingers, and on the fourth finger, I had a revelation. There was someone else who might know, someone who must have known about our family's secret for years. I lifted a fifth finger. "The shark!"

"Um, Aileen, I don't think a shark can—"

"No! That guy who wants to buy my dad's store. He and my mom used to date in high school. A couple of weeks ago, he mentioned something about my mom being a champion swimmer, that she could out-swim a shark. He *must* have known what she was." The more I thought about it, the more it made sense. "He arrived in town just before the attacks started. He's got tons of money, and his offer

162

went up after the attacks on Deirdre and Bridget. He's buying up all the shops to build his own store. What if he wants to use his store as a front for *other* things?" I yanked open the front pocket of my backpack where I still had his card. *Ben Harwood. Entrepreneur. Dealer of art and antiquities.*

Jamie's eyes popped open. "Antiquities. I have a feeling I know what that means."

"That's it, then!" Ben had known what my mom was in high school, but he probably hadn't learned about the skins until he moved away and became interested in "antiquities." He'd come back with a plan to set up a home base and increase his fortune, skin by skin. But he didn't plan on us figuring anything out, even though he practically *told* us. *This town needs to be cleaned up, and in order to do that, there have to be certain casualties.* We had him, and I couldn't wait to see him rot in jail for every person he had ever touched.

Jamie squeezed my hands. "I'll be back soon I promise."

"Hurry, please."

"I will." He leaned in to kiss me, his lips soft against mine. Vulnerable. Afraid. Just like me. He pulled back a fraction of an inch, far enough that he wasn't technically kissing me, but close enough that his lips still brushed against mine when he spoke. I didn't want him to stop, but he had to go. "I really care about you. Whatever happens, don't forget that."

"I won't."

After one last kiss, he took off through the scrub, and soon I heard the splash of him diving into the water.

In the distance, thunder rumbled.

A thin river of water trickled in through the mouth of the cave, pooling into a small puddle near my feet. The tang of ozone and rain scented the air. The storm wasn't bad yet, but judging by the dark, angry clouds filling the sky, it was just getting started. The sun was nearly gone, escaping the day like I wished I could.

I had done nothing but pace the length of the cave since Jamie left. He had been gone for hours. Why wasn't he back yet?

As the minutes ticked by, my thoughts had untangled from a thick, jumbled mess into something slightly more coherent. I regretted not grabbing my phone out of my room. During The Moment, the thought never crossed my mind, but now, more than anything I wanted to call my parents. To tell them I was okay. Had they come home yet? If so, what did they find? Jamie would've called them, right? Warned them? He said he was going to get help, but what did that mean exactly? They never called the police for Bridget.

God, why hadn't I asked what he meant by "help?"

Guilt gnawed at my stomach. Why hadn't I insisted on calling my parents first? If I was in danger, so was my mom.

I raked my hands through my hair, hearing the pop of hairs coming lose from my scalp. I had to get out of here.

My pack sat on a rock shelf near the back of the cave. I'd stuck it there when it started raining. Not that it mattered if it got wet. It was just something to do. Now, I got down on my hands and knees and searched for a better place to hide it. Jamie said he used a number of different caves to hide his skin; there had to be a hole here somewhere. The dying light made seeing difficult, but I had never been too squeamish about bugs and stuff, so I poked my hands behind each rock and felt around until I found one that didn't connect with solid ground. The rock was bigger than something I would normally try to lift, but I put my shoulder into it and got it a few inches away from the back wall.

I stuck my hand behind the rock, finding a deep hole. Jackpot.

With a little more sweat and determination, I got my pack in there, replaced the rock, and was soon heading for the boat. The sky had darkened even more, but the heavy rain was still a good distance away. I could make it. I hoped.

Before long, I was in the water, rowing. It was a lot more difficult than Jamie made it look. Or maybe I hadn't been paying attention. Either way, I was glad to be moving, not pacing, not waiting. I didn't know what I'd do once I got home, but I tried not to think about it. I focused on the rowing. And the rain.

The cold drops plunked harder on my face. I tried to blink them away, but as the storm moved in, I found myself stopping every minute or so to wipe my face with my shirt. It didn't take long for the fabric to soak, but it was better than nothing. Maybe leaving hadn't been such a good idea after all, but I couldn't turn around. The wind pushed through me, blowing me forward.

As I approached the bigger island, the waves showed their anger by lapping over the edges of the boat. The oars grew slick from the water, and I struggled to hold on to them, barely managing to row. With each pull of the oars, my biceps screamed, and my throat burned with heavy breaths.

"Keep going. Keep going," I chanted to myself.

White caps formed on the waves, and the rain stung like ice chunks against my skin. I rounded the bigger island, expecting to see my house, but I couldn't see twenty feet away. Panic filled my senses. Was I even going in the right direction? I swung my head around. Clumps of sopping wet hair plastered themselves to my face. Waves knocked the boat, spinning it in circles, nauseating and disorienting me. I looked for the island I had just passed, but even it had disappeared in the storm.

My heart hammered against my ribs, seeking an escape. I had to get out of this, get back to an island somehow. The big one, the little one, it didn't matter.

Lightning flashed over the ocean. The hairs on my arms stood up, and thunder deafened my ears. I dug the oars into the water and turned the boat, guessing at the direction. As I did that, a wave crashed over the side, flooding the bottom with a foot of water and knocking me off balance. In my panic, I dropped the oars and gripped the sides of the boat. It was all I could do to hold on, never mind reaching for the oars which were now lost to the ocean.

"Help!" I screamed, though to who I could only guess. The selkies? Mermaids? Poseidon himself? I was willing to believe they were all real if only someone would come help me.

Rain and tears poured down my face, a mixture of hot and cold, making my teeth chatter and my face burn. Another wave crashed over me. And another one. And another. With each deluge, the boat came closer and closer to capsizing. I couldn't hold on to the sides any longer. My hands were too wet and my fingers too sore.

"Please, please, ple—" My cries cut off as I watched the largest wave yet coming straight for me. There would be no escaping this one. A strange sense of calm settled over me, and I realized my mother was right. The sea was coming to claim me. I squeezed my eyes shut, waiting, waiting, waiting . . .

# Chapter Twenty

"Aileen!"

My eyes popped open at the sound of his voice. It couldn't be.

"Dad? Daddy???"

The wave hit, knocking the boat over and dumping me into the water. I went under, my lungs burning as I gulped water. I kicked and flailed not knowing which way was up, but refusing to give up. Not when I knew what I had heard.

I kept kicking, and finally a rope tangled around my arm. The rope from the rowboat! I grabbed hold of it and slowly, arm over arm, pulled myself up beside the overturned boat. When I surfaced, I flung my arms over the hull. The rain and waves clawed at me, but Mont's boat was so close. I could see its shadowy form approaching through the storm. I hacked and coughed, spewing water everywhere.

"Daddy!" I tried to scream. My throat was so raw, it was hard to tell how far my voice carried. "Over here!"

"There!" someone shouted. "I see a boat! Aileen?"

*Yes! Yes, it's me!* I couldn't tell if I said it out loud or not. It didn't matter. They saw me. I forced in breath after breath, all the while keeping my death grip on the boat. They were coming! Oh thank God, they were coming! As Mont's boat pulled up beside me and he threw down the anchor, I dropped my forehead onto the hull, closed my eyes, and cried with relief.

I heard a splash, then felt the sharp tug of arms hauling me out of the water and up to the boat. Blankets wrapped around me and more arms carried me someplace dry and soft. They called my name, patted my face. I burrowed deeper under the covers, wanting to give in to unconsciousness. Oblivion.

"Aileen, baby, come on." Daddy sounded so worried. So scared. I had to tell him that I was . . . what? That I was all right? No. That I was still here? Yes, maybe that would do.

I rubbed my face against the blanket and opened my eyes. Mont's cabin was a blurry haze, and my eyes stung like they had been scraped with sandpaper. The boat rocked viciously, pumping the nausea out of my stomach and up my throat. I twisted the top half of my body over the side of the bed where Mont held a bucket ready for me.

I might've thrown up a gallon of salt water. It was hard to tell. But when the burning and the heaving were done with, I collapsed back onto the bed where my dad hovered over me, dabbing my face with a towel and kissing my forehead.

"Oh, baby. Don't ever scare me like that again."

*I won't.* The words wouldn't come out until I cleared my throat with a cough. "I won't. But Daddy? Something terrible happened."

"We know." He leaned so close to me, like a parent cooing over a newborn child. His thumb brushed the strands of damp hair away from my face. He squeezed his eyes shut, and a few tears dropped down onto the blanket. He *did* know. I was glad I didn't have to say it out loud.

I fisted my hand in his shirt and pulled him closer. "Listen to me. Fee wasn't the first. There's someone hunting selkies for their skins, and Mom could be in danger too."

Dad untangled my fingers from his shirt and held my hand in both of his. "Your mom is safe. She's with the police now."

"Great! I need to talk to them. I know who did it. It's that guy who—" I stopped because I saw my dad give Mont a knowing look, the kind that says they don't know if they're going to let you in on the secret or not. "What?" I hated it when my parents did that, and I hated it now. "Tell me!"

Mont spoke first. "We already know who's responsible."

"Your friend Ian called me," Dad clarified.

I pushed myself up on my elbows. The boat lurched again, and my stomach roiled. Lightning flashed through the skylight, highlighting the way my dad wasn't looking at me. "But how would he know? He wasn't even there."

"He never made it in the house," my dad said gently. "He stopped by to see you and saw them arguing through the front window."

"Fee and Ben?"

"Fee and Liam Flannigan."

I blinked, certain I'd heard the wrong name. Or maybe he had misunderstood the question. "What does he have to do with this?"

"The Flannigans are murderers." Mont spoke simply and abruptly. "That man lost his temper, and I'm willing to bet that boy of his knew something about it."

"No!" I sat bolt upright. My head split open with pain. I pressed my palms against my eyes to stop the throbbing. "No, Jamie was with me when we found her, and he was just as devastated as I was. He was the one who wanted me to hide. To protect me because I'm one of them."

"Just like I 'spected," Mont said to my dad.

Dad muttered an agreement, and I slammed my fist down onto the bed.

"Stop talking around me. I'm right here!"

"Sweetie," my dad put his hand on my shoulder. "We believe Jamie took you. He was hiding you until his family had the chance to smuggle you out of town."

Mont growled. "I told you they'd hide her out on one of those islands. They did it before, and they did it again."

No, he had done it to help me. To protect me. "But he called the police, didn't he? To tell them about . . . about . . ."

Dad slowly shook his head. "After Ian called, I went straight home, and I found your grandmother. I called the police. They took Ian's statement and then searched the Flannigan's property. Jamie and his family are gone. Their house has been abandoned."

I felt like a giant rubber band was wrapped around my chest, squeezing tighter and tighter. It couldn't be true. Jamie had promised to call someone. He said he cared about me. But a niggling feeling reminded me he'd clarified that statement. *Whatever happens* . . . What did he expect to happen? "What was the argument about?"

"You. He said you belonged with them," Mont spat out the words like they were poisoned. "He said she would regret taking you from them."

"Do you know where Jamie is now?" my dad asked. "Did he say anything to you today about his family?"

I searched my mind for anything. Thunder rattled the boat. The raging storm seeped into my mind. It hurt to think. It hurt to breathe. Jamie couldn't have betrayed me like that. "He said they had to go. Relocate."

"Did he give you a reason?"

"It's not safe for them here. He said most of his family left. His father stayed to take care of some business, and Jamie wanted to say goodbye to me."

"Business." Mont hissed the word. "Guess we know what that means."

"Stop it!" I said. "Jamie wouldn't . . . Jamie didn't . . ." He cared about me. The Flannigans had been so kind to me, like I was a part of them. "It *can't* be them."

Mont shook his head, disbelief etched in every line of his face. "Selkies is horrible creatures. I've told you time and again, they act without remorse."

"No," I said as my arms gave out from me and I collapsed onto the pillow. My head felt like it was still submerged underwater. Blues and blacks swam before my eyes, a nightmare come to life, engulfing me and dragging me under. My lungs ached for air that couldn't be found. "No."

Dad touched my arm, and I pulled it away, shoving both hands under the covers. "Sweetie, I know this is hard for you."

I pulled the blanket over my head. "Just go away."

"Aileen, please—"

"Go! Away!" I shouted over another crash of thunder.

I felt his weight shift off the bed, muffled footsteps, and the click of the door as the two of them left me to figure out how I was ever gonna breathe again.

# Chapter Twenty-One

By the time we got back, it was dark out. The rain had slowed, but Dad and Mont had bundled me in three layers of blankets for the trek from our pier to the house. I didn't fight it, though I doubted a thousand blankets could stop the cold feeling from slicing at my insides.

They led me in the back door, making sure to block my view of the living room as we made our way to the kitchen. The bright light hurt my eyes and made my head throb, so I hovered in the doorway. Mom sat at the table, her face buried in her hands, wet streaks running down her fingers. Ian sat at the table as well, his arms folded across his chest as he glared at Hansel and Rowe.

Ian grumbled to the policemen. "I've told you everything I heard. I left before any—"

I took a small step forward. "Mommy?"

I saw her face for a second, red and blotchy and soaked with tears. "Oh my God." Then, she was wrapped around me, both of us shaking and sobbing. She pressed her hand against the back of my head, holding me tight to her shoulder. "What were you thinking? Don't you ever do that again, do you hear me?" She pulled away to look me in the eye, but there was no anger there. Only fear and overwhelming sadness. And a lot of it was my fault.

"I won't," I said. "I promise."

She squeezed me once more, and as soon as she released me, Ian grabbed me up in a strong hug lifting my feet in the air. Just as quickly, he let go and backed away, his eyes trained on the floor.

"I'm um . . . glad you're okay."

"Thanks," I said as my mom helped me over to the table. I didn't know what else to say. A few weeks ago, I wouldn't have expected to see him anywhere near my house. But now, it seemed perfectly natural, and that surprised me. Did that mean we were friends again? I didn't have the energy to think about it past that.

My mom hovered over me, smoothing my hair and rubbing my arms. After a minute or two, I sunk forward onto the table, my weight supported on shaky arms. She mumbled something about fixing some tea. I didn't particularly want tea, but I was cold and my throat hurt, so I didn't argue.

While Mom fussed with the kettle, Hansel addressed me, the tip of his pen clacking against the table. "So, Miss Shay, tell us what you know about the Flannigans."

I opened my mouth to answer, but all that came out was a loud hiccupping sob. And soon I had my face buried in my hands just like my mom had been doing when I walked in.

My mom slammed a spoon down on the counter. "Alex, get them out of here. She's had enough for tonight."

"Gentlemen," Dad said, "let's talk outside."

Chairs scraped the linoleum and boots tromped across the floor. My mom knelt beside me, rubbing her hand back and forth across my back. I tucked my head against her neck.

"I'm sorry," I whispered. "Mom, I'm so sorry."

"Shh, baby." I felt her warm breath against my cheek. It reminded me of nights when I was little, and she'd rock me to sleep. "It's my fault. I knew you were too young to—"

I pulled away from her. Whatever comfort I'd just felt evaporated in a hot steam. "I'm not too young. I'm sixteen years old. I'm not a child."

Mom pushed herself to her feet, her hands moving to her hips in a stance I was all too familiar with. The only difference was this time she had to fist away a tear from her cheek before speaking. "Well, you certainly haven't proven it. The second I gave you some freedom, you ran away and nearly got yourself killed."

"I made a mistake. I know that. It's not gonna happen again."

"How do I know that? How do I know you're not going to take off into the water whenever you want chasing some idealized dream of what your life should be?"

"Because I can't!" I pushed the blankets off of me and stood up. "The skin is gone!"

Mom stopped, long enough to lower her voice an octave. Never a good thing. "What are you saying?"

"It's lost." And as far as I was concerned, that was the truth. I never wanted to see that thing again. Not when it symbolized the most horrible things that had ever happened in my life. "The ocean can have it."

Her mouth dropped open, but no sound came out. A full minute ticked by on the kitchen clock. "It . . . it's really gone?"

I nodded once, firmly. "Forever."

As we stood there, me wanting to curl up into a fetal ball and Mom sorting out how next to yell at me, the kettle began to whistle, its sound cutting through the thick air.

From the doorway, Mont cleared his throat. "I can get that."

Mom moved over to the stove. "No, I will." She slid the kettle off the burner and dropped it onto a hot pad. But instead of busying herself with the cup and sugar bowl like I expected her to do, she turned around and sagged back against the stove. She ran her hands through her hair, dragging it away from her face. Had she always looked that . . . tired? "Did you need something, Mont?"

"No, ma'am." He leaned against the door frame. His fishing cap was a ball in his weathered hands. "I was just saying g'night. Alex has got things settled with the police, and the young man has gone home. I wanted to see if you needed anything 'fore I left."

Mom sighed. "No. We do appreciate your help though."

"All right then." He gave a small salute. "I'll be taking off."

"Night."

As soon as we heard the back door shut, Mom straightened up and put on her "we need to talk" face. "Aileen—"

I held up my hand. I was tired of fighting. "I'm going to bed. It's been a long day."

"Wait. I think we should—"

"No," I said. "We really shouldn't."

I curled up in my bed and lay there sulking until my phone vibrated. Mae texting me.

*Where r u? Please answer. Ur parents have me rly scared.*

I scrolled through my messages. There were half a dozen from Mae, a couple from my parents as well as several voice mails, and four from Ian.

I texted Mae back, *Im fine Call u later.*

But I wasn't fine. A long way from it.

I sucked in a courage builder and typed a message to Jamie. It consisted of three words:

*Did your dad . . .*

I hit send and less than a minute later, I got my answer.

*I'm sorry,* he said.

And that was it.

Fresh tears stung my eyes. "Dammit!" I wiped them away with the back of my wrist. No one in that family deserved my tears. Fee had trusted them, and they'd betrayed her. They were monsters just like Mont had always said.

And if the Flannigans were capable of doing . . . that, then I was willing to bet they were responsible for Bridget and Deirdre too. Jamie's dad was furious when he found out about Kyle.

*I refuse to let her end up like Deirdre.* That's what Mrs. Flannigan had said to her husband.

Was taking Bridget's skin and attacking her a form of punishment? It was certainly a way to ensure she'd never see Kyle again, and a warning sent out to everyone at that bonfire. Deirdre screwed up, and Bridget apparently hadn't learned from that lesson. She needed the point drilled home.

*They's soulless creatures.*

That cabin. Bridget's parents had isolated her there. I'd thought it was for protection, but what if it was for something else? She seemed so different from the first time I'd seen her. Like she'd given up. Had her dad done that to her?

*They act without remorse.*

Deirdre had hated being a selkie. She'd threatened to run away. What if she had? And the only way to ensure she wouldn't do it again was to make sure she couldn't.

*They bring nothing but heartache.*

Jamie stuck me in a cave, expecting me to be too scared to leave. Trapping me there. Stealing my family, piece by horrible piece.

Mr. Glenn and my dad had never been able to find the attackers because they'd been searching in the wrong places. I should have known. I should have told someone. I hadn't, and now my grandma was gone.

I chucked my phone across the room and stomped over to my desk where I kept my drawings of Jamie's eyes. I'd planned on framing one or two of them, so I could stare into his eyes whenever I wanted. Not surprisingly, the appeal had gone. I ripped the pictures into confetti and dumped them in my garbage can. Then I stuck the can outside my door, hoping someone would take care of it for me. I didn't want to see that trash ever again.

# Chapter Twenty-Two

The morning of Fee's funeral dawned a murky gray. It seemed appropriate, the way the sky reflected the dark clouds stirring inside of me. The sun hadn't come out since her death three days before. Rowe and Hansel had approached me several times, but I couldn't tell them anything they didn't already know. They suspected she was hit over the head with one of our lighthouse statues. Mom had told them it was missing, and it was about the right size. They searched the house for it, though it was probably down at the bottom of the ocean by now.

With Ian's statement combined with mine, the police put out a state-wide hunt for the Flannigans. They wouldn't find them. They wouldn't know where to look. And what was I supposed to say? Check the ocean? They would have patted me on the head and sent me off to a doctor to scan for brain injuries. So I was left to stew in my own misery, knowing they would never be caught.

The service was simple. We couldn't afford a viewing or a proper service, so we all sat in folding chairs under a blue canopy at the cemetery. My family. Our friends. A man in a dark suit said some nice words, called her a good Christian woman, though she'd never attended church, and we all prayed. People cried, they held hands, and when the talking was over, the cemetery people made us leave so they could put my grandmother in the ground.

Before anyone could stop me, I took off, disappearing among the tombstones. To clear out the mental noise, I studied the random names and dates, wondering who they were, making up stories about their lives. Eventually I came to a bench. It was small and wooden, with a memorial plaque rubbed flat by the years. I sat down and looked out over the grounds, unsure what to do next.

"Not trying to run away again, are you?"

I looked up just in time to see Mae plopping down beside me.

"I didn't run away the first time," I grumbled.

"I know," she said softly. She knew everything, minus the selkie part. After Sunday night when I'd woken up screaming every hour, Mom had agreed to let me stay with her. I just couldn't face normal life in my own house right now. I couldn't deal with final exams. Hell, I couldn't deal with getting out of bed and seeing the living room, minus the large, oval rug. After the coroner had come, Dad had thrown the rug in the back of his truck and driven away with it. But its absence was just as much a reminder as the blood stains.

I twisted the Claddagh rings on my right hand, Fee's on my ring finger, and Grandpa Colm's on my thumb. My mom had wanted me to go home with her and dad tonight, but I doubted she would force me. "Do you mind if I stay at your house for a few more days? Just til the end of the week." Staying there, I could fool myself enough to get through the waking hours. Pretend I was there on a sleepover. And when it came time to sleep, well, my mom had given me pills for that.

"Of course. Stay as long as you want."

"Thank you."

We were silent for a few minutes. The clouds pressed further down in the sky, and I wondered how long it would be before I saw the sun. But even then, there would still be shadows and darkness to deal with.

"Why?" I asked Mae, knowing I wouldn't have to elaborate.

She considered it for a while, then gave me a very definite, "Because."

"O-kay then."

Just because.

I didn't like the answer at first, because it didn't contain some magical cure. I couldn't rub on a lotion that suddenly made my heart feel lighter. My days easier. It didn't delete the pain or even dull the edges. But the more I thought about it, the more I realized sometimes "because" was the only answer you got. It was certainly better than my mom's answer, which was to let out a string of curse words and then excuse herself from the room. Or my dad, who would give me a hug and start to sing something he thought was appropriate. No, out of everyone, Mae's answer was definitely the best. I managed a weak smile. "Thanks. You're a good friend."

"No," she scoffed. "I'm your BFF. There's a huge difference. Worlds apart. Maybe even a universe or two."

And of course I laughed. "At least."

"Good," she said with a smile. "I'm glad you agree."

She slid her arm around me, and as I dropped my head to her shoulder, some of the tension dropped out of me. Or maybe I let it go. Whatever the case, it felt good. There were a lot of reasons Mae and I were friends, and her ability to put things in perspective was one of them.

"Aw, are we having a moment?" Ian sang from behind us.

"Yep," I said, scooting over so Steven could squeeze in beside Mae. Ian perched on the arm rest beside me.

"Milkshakes at the diner?" Steven asked. "Our treat."

Mae looked hopefully at me. "You up for it?"

"Sure," I said. It might do me good to hang out.

Just because.

"Great, let's go!" She popped out of the seat and dragged Steven back to the path, babbling a mile a minute. I followed after, but Ian touched my arm to stop me.

"Can we talk?"

"Um . . . sure." I looked pointedly at his hand which was still touching my arm. I didn't mind it so much. It just felt weird. Like the hug in my kitchen. I didn't think we did that sort of thing.

He removed it and brushed his palm against his pants. "Sorry."

I lifted one shoulder in a shrug. "Don't worry about it." I started walking again, but slower this time. "What's up?"

"I'm sorry."

"You've already said that."

"No. About Sunday."

I stopped. It felt like he had just nailed me in the stomach with a baseball. Why was he talking about this? It was done. It was over.

But he kept talking. "I should have done something. Knocked on the door. Called the police. I could have stopped it."

"Don't." I squeezed my eyes shut against the sharp pain shooting from my shoulders down to my toes. Just breathe. It would pass. It always did. "Forget it, okay?"

"Aileen, look at me. Please?"

I lifted my eyes. He was standing right in front of me, just as breathless and just as miserable. But he would get over it. I didn't blame him for what happened. If I had never gotten involved with Jamie, then his family would never have come for me. Or maybe I thought that because blaming myself was so damned easy.

I took a couple of hurried steps down the path, mostly to distance myself from the conversation. "Let's just go. They're probably at the cars by now."

"I know what you are."

I froze. My heart skittered up into my throat. He knew? He *knew?*

"My dad told me. *Just* me."

Oh, well then. That made *everything* better. *Way to go, Ian. Why don't you poke at everything that's raw and painful inside of me?* I brushed him off with a wave of my hand, hoping he didn't notice how I trembled. "I'm not anything. Not anymore."

"He and his friend in the government, they watch the selkies to protect them. Your dad was helping too. They had no idea the Flannigans were actually responsible. He thinks Jamie told you they were being hunted to throw off—"

"Ian." I needed him to stop.

"Aileen." He stepped closer. Too close. His words brushed hot against my neck. "You can talk to me about this. I'll listen. I want to help."

Why didn't he understand? I didn't want to talk about it. I wanted it all to go away as quickly as possible. And if that didn't happen, I would drown it so deep it would never surface again. "You know what? I'm not hungry anymore. Tell Mae I'll see her back at her house."

And I ran. I couldn't get away from there fast enough.

When Mae got home, she found me laying on her bedroom floor, my history book and notes spread out around me. I wasn't actually looking at them. I was imagining the info creeping into me by osmosis.

Mae dropped down beside me with a scowl on her face. She said Ian had bailed on them. He wouldn't explain why, but he looked really upset.

"Well, that makes two of us," I said.

She grabbed my ancient phone off my air mattress and tossed it to me.

I caught it before it smashed to the floor and it broke apart for about the millionth time. I really needed a new phone. "What do you expect me to do with this?"

"Fix it. He just wants to do something. He feels terrible."

"It's not his fault." I wrapped my phone charm around one of my fingers until the tip of my finger turned white. "There's nothing he *can* do."

"Are you sure?"

"Of course I'm sure. He can't—" I stopped myself as Ian's offer to help took on a new meaning. He didn't have the resources to do anything, but maybe his father did. If Mr. Glenn knew about the Flannigans . . . If he had contacts in the government . . .

I untangled my finger and punched in a text to Ian. *If u rly want 2 help, have ur dad find them.* And then because I felt bad I'd hurt his feelings, I added. *Please.*

A moment later a text came back. *He's on it.*

"There," I said, setting my phone on the floor beside me. "Satisfied?"

"Nope." And before I could protest, she sent him another text. *Im really sry I ran away frm u.*

*4given?*

"Hey!" I snatched my phone back, but he had already replied. *Nothing to forgive.*

And for some reason, that made me smile.

# Chapter Twenty-Three

I went home that weekend. A lot of good it did me. I spent two days staring out of my window at the water. Funny how it used to comfort me. Now the sound of the waves made me feel like I was running my ears through a blender. Yet I couldn't take my eyes away.

I was looking for something.

On Sunday night, I saw it. A sleek, brown seal bottling about twenty feet in the water, watching my house. I jumped out of my window and ran through the dunes.

"Hey! HEY!" I raced toward the water, my worn out sneakers slipping through the dry sand. "What do think you're doing?" I screamed as I stumbled down to the water's edge. "Get up here! Get up here and face what you've done!"

He stared for a second longer, then ducked under the water and disappeared.

I waited for five minutes, ten minutes. And when he didn't resurface, I balled my fists and shouted, "Coward!"

Back in my room, I texted Ian.

*He was here. In the water.*

He texted back.

*I'll tell my dad. Don't go out there alone.*

I got through the last few days of school, history exam and all. I was pretty sure I passed, though I doubted with anything better than a C. Now I just had to face summer break. I could do it, hopefully without looking over my shoulder every five minutes to see if *he* was there. And if he did show up, it was equal bets on whether I would run away or punch him in the face. Oh, who was I kidding? I would definitely punch him.

Dad called, asking me to stop by Fish Tales one afternoon so he could get some work done in his office. I didn't mind. Again, it made life seem normal. But when he handed me a pricing gun and told me to start marking down the entire wall of sparkly rubber bait, I threw a fit. I knew what came after marking down the merchandise.

"No, we're not clearancing anything out!" We had to have money. Dad promised us he had a plan. "You were working for Mr. Glenn. I saw you, so don't try to deny it. He had to have paid you, right?"

Dad shook his head. "Our job was to catch whoever was stealing the selkie skins. We didn't do that, so we didn't get paid. I'm signing over the store in a week."

"So we still have time! Maybe Mr. Glenn could give us a loan. And if not, we'll find another way!"

"Please," he closed his eyes like Mom always did when she had a headache, "just do it. Twenty-five percent off."

"No!" I dropped the gun on the counter, and grabbed his wrist, attempting to drag him toward the office. "They're not taking our store. We'll get the money from somewhere."

"Aileen, it's too late."

"Come on." Why wasn't he moving? Were his feet glued to the ground? "I'll help you look. Two pairs of eyes are better than one, right?"

He yanked his hand from mine. "Aileen, stop it! We're broke! It's the end of the month! There's nothing we can do!"

I stopped, frozen, with no idea how to respond. His shout rattled in my ears. My dad didn't yell at me like that. Ever.

Dad grabbed the pricing gun from the counter and, without looking at me, stuffed it back in my hands. "Twenty-five percent off." And then he walked back into his office and shut the door.

I did what I was told, but as soon as I was done, I grabbed my stuff and left. I didn't bother saying goodbye. What was the point? He'd probably just yell at me again.

As I unlocked my bike from the bike rack, I noticed the pitiful state of Paws by the Sea. The rhinestone collars and designer bowls were absent from their window display. The paintings I'd done for them had been stripped from the walls; they'd been sold right along with the shelves and fixtures. Only a few things remained for pick-up, and the sign out front said it was by appointment only.

Scotty Laplace, a senior in my high school, pushed a broom around the empty floor. The owners had moved to California last week, leaving Scotty to take care of things. I wondered how long it would be before that was me, sweeping away the remains of my dad's dream.

"Hey! I was hoping I'd see you." Ian popped out of his car and ran up to me.

I dropped my bike onto the sidewalk. For a moment I forgot about the store and allowed my body to tingle with hope. "Did your dad find them?" I'd emailed him the photos I'd taken of the Jamie seal along with any photos I had of the seals that hung out with him.

"Not yet," he said. "But he doesn't think Jamie's here anymore. A pod of seals, including one matching his description, was spotted up near Cannon Beach. My dad's gone up there today to check on them."

"Okay, thanks." Out of the corner of my eye, I caught sight of my dad taping a large piece of cardboard in our store window. I shouldn't have looked, but I did. My voice shook as I read the words, "Going Out of Business Sale," scrawled in black Sharpie.

"Dammit!" I kicked the tire on my bike. Of course that was a mistake because, "Ow." And whether it was Jamie stalking me, the sign, the throbbing in my little toe, or a combination of them all, a familiar prickling formed behind my eyes. I covered my face with my hands, because I didn't want Ian to see me cry, and I couldn't think of anywhere to run.

"Hey, don't." Ian pulled me into his arms. "Come here. It'll be okay."

"No, it won't," I mumbled against his chest. "We're broke. Dad's selling the store. What's gonna happen next? Are we gonna lose the house?"

"Don't even think about that. If it ever came down to it, I'd steal my dad's boat and sell it on eBay for you guys." He pulled back so I could see the mischievous twinkle in his eyes. "You know I'd do it too."

I almost laughed, but before I got the chance, inspiration struck. The kind that appears out of nowhere, and makes you wonder why you never thought of it before. "Ian, you're a genius!"

He gave me a "You just figured that out" look that quickly turned into a confused one. "Well, of course I am. But does this mean you expect me to steal my dad's boat?"

"No. I mean yes, but not to sell it on eBay. I just need a ride." I pulled myself out of his arms and bent down to reset the lock on my bike. I fumbled it because my hands were shaking so badly. This was going to work. It had to.

"Okay." He bent down and closed the lock for me. "But if I'm going to incur my dad's wrath, can you at least tell me where we're going?"

"I need you to take me to one of the islands," I said, grabbing his hand and pulling him down the street toward the docks. "I left something there."

# Chapter Twenty-Four

Fee said you could give your skin away without any real repercussions. Well, that's what I was going to do, only the taker would be funding my dad's store in return. Mr. Glenn may not have been selling selkie skins, but if he was working with the government, he had to have connections. He'd know someone. And since selling your own skin wasn't technically illegal, it wouldn't be a problem, right?

Added bonus? The Flannigans would no longer have any reason to stalk me.

Ian "conveniently" had a spare key to the *Speedy Little Devil* on his key chain. It was one of those designer keys, and it had a picture of The Beatles and a cartoon yellow submarine on it. I gave him a look when he pulled it out, one that said *Really?* His face twisted up into a grin.

In less than five minutes, Ian was at the wheel, steering us out of the slip. I was standing beside him, pointing to the big island that hid the smaller one where my bag was hidden.

"That way," I said.

"Okay."

His dad's speedboat would have had us there in less than a minute if we could've opened it up, but since we were still in the bay and had to go slooow, it was taking quite a bit longer. I danced at his side, my fingers gripping the windshield as we crept toward the big island. I wanted to get there and get this over with.

Then, figure out what to do next.

It turned out there were at least a dozen little islands behind the larger one, and having spent most of my time there in a cave, they all looked the same to me. I searched one after the other, each time jumping down into an orange inflatable life raft and rowing myself to shore. Ian had to anchor the boat in chest deep water, and I couldn't walk up from there. It was too cold, and the currents were fairly strong.

After a couple of hours, the sun dissolved into a faint, pink line on the horizon, and as I picked my way through the scrub on the fourth island, I wondered for the millionth time why I hadn't paid more attention when Jamie brought me out here. Of course I knew the answer. Because my life had been falling apart. Because absolutely everything had gone wrong.

As the branches scraped my arms and tore holes in my shirt, I reminded myself I was here to change all that. Getting my skin back and getting rid of it wasn't going to fix everything, but it would fix something. That would have to be enough for now.

I was about to give up on that island when I pushed aside a branch and saw the dark mouth of a very familiar cave.

"Yes!"

The skin was right where I left it. I hadn't wanted to admit it, but I'd been a little afraid Jamie had come out here and taken it. He could have, thinking I'd be forced to go with them. He probably knew exactly where it was. But it was here, and it was safe. I cradled the pack in my arms and worked my way back to the bright orange raft and finally to the speedboat.

I threw my pack onto the boat, and Ian took my hand to help me climb in. Once we got the raft stowed, he picked up my bag. The zipper was partially open, and it was obvious what was inside.

He started to hand it to me, then paused, his fingers touching the zipper, but not moving it. "Do you mind?"

"Oh, um, sure. Go ahead."

He unzipped it the rest of the way and pulled out the skin, laying it flat on the deck of the boat. He was careful, reverential, as if it were his own. He knelt beside it, gently touching one of the front flippers. "Have you . . ."

It felt weird having him look at it, that part of me. Hell, it felt weird for *me* to look at it. My chest seized up with longing, something I hadn't expected. I was going to sell it. It was no longer mine to want. "Once."

Ian looked up at me, amazement in his eyes. "What's it like?"

Horrible. Terrifying. At least the things that went with it. The swimming itself was, "Magic."

The pain in my chest crept up my throat and burned. I faced the ocean, willing it to stop speaking to me. I didn't want to think about the magic. It was gone. It *had* to be.

For my dad.

Ian came to stand beside me. He was so quiet when he spoke. "Do you think you could show me sometime. Is that allowed?"

Absolutely not. I would never swim again, not as Aileen and certainly not as that seal. "I don't know what the rules are anymore." No. No! I was supposed to have said no. It was that damn skin's fault. I bent down and shoved it back in the bag. I didn't bother zipping it; I tossed it in the corner to get it away from me.

"Aileen, what's—"

"We should get the boat back. I don't want you to get in trouble."

He paused, his eyes asking a question I couldn't answer. "Um, sure. Okay."

Without another word, I began pulling up the anchor. He moved to the front, and as soon as I gave him the all clear, he pushed up on the throttle. The engine sputtered out. He turned the key. This time, nothing happened.

"Um . . ." He turned the key several more times, checked a couple of gauges, flipped a couple of switches. "Yeah, we're not going anywhere. I think we're just out of fuel. I'm not sure though. It could be something more."

"Uh oh." I looked at the dials on the dashboard, thinking I would be able to see something he couldn't. Like I knew how to fix a boat.

He banged his fist on the side of the boat. "Dammit! My dad's gonna kill me!"

"No! It's my fault! I won't let you take the blame. We'll just . . . um . . ." I spotted the radio hanging from the dash. "We'll call for help. Your dad's not on a boat, right? He won't hear you on the hailing channel?"

"No, but we can't call the Coast Guard. My dad knows people."

"We won't. I know who to call." I grabbed the mic. "*Nereid's Storm. Nereid's Storm. Nereid's Storm.* This is *Aileen's Wish.* Over." I didn't mention our actual boat name, just in case.

The answer crackled through the speaker. "*Aileen's Wish.* This is *Nereid's Storm.* Over."

"Switch to channel sixty-eight. Over." We switched to a private channel, and I explained the situation.

Mont mumbled something about my dad not being too happy with me if he ever found out, but said he'd be there with help in less than an hour.

I thanked him, then Ian and I plopped down in the white, leather seats at the back of the boat to wait.

The sun was mostly down, and the night air held a chill. Ian noticed when I rubbed the goose bumps off my arm and reached into a storage box for a blanket. It was small, but comfy.

"Thanks," I said.

He shrugged. "It's just a blanket."

"No." How could I explain this? "I mean, thank you for everything. I wasn't thinking. I should have asked Mont to do this. Not you."

"Don't. There's a reason I have a key to this boat, and it wasn't because of you." A mischievous smile spread across his face as he slid down in his seat and tilted his head back against the headrest. He laced his fingers across his stomach and sighed. "I am who I am. On a night like this, I may have taken the boat out even if you hadn't asked." He flopped his head to the side, directing his smile at me. "You coming along is just a perk."

"Oh." I met his gaze evenly, and I liked what I saw there, someone who made no apologies for who he was, someone who hid nothing.

He touched his fingertips to mine, and tugged my hand off the seat, so our arms were swinging between us, barely touching. His skin was soft and warm. "You know, maybe we should hang out sometime when it doesn't involve a felony."

"Like a date?"

"Yeah. If you want." His thumb traced over one of my fingernails.

I thought about pulling away, but my body wouldn't respond. I don't think it wanted to. The truth was I didn't know what I wanted from him. Friends or something else. Whatever it was, it hurt to think about it, because my insides felt too raw from what Jamie had done. I needed time to adjust. "My parents are gonna find out about this, and I'll probably be grounded until infinity."

He dropped his hand, letting it dangle at his side, and frowned up at the stars. "Don't make excuses, Aileen. If you don't want to, I get it. I just thought maybe you'd give me another chance. We're not in middle school anymore."

Great. How many more ways was I going to screw up with him? I wanted him in my life. I just didn't know how.

"Ian." I touched his forearm. "That wasn't a no. It was my way of saying, 'Ask me again once it's over.'"

He looked down at my fingers, studying them, then lifted his gaze to mine. My breath stumbled from the unexpected rush that shot through me. Different from what I'd felt with Jamie, but still good.

We stayed locked in that moment, frozen until the sound of an approaching boat broke between us.

"It's Mont," I said, jumping to my feet.

Ian headed toward the front of the boat, while I stayed near the back to help tie the two boats together. As soon as that was done, Kyle and his friend, I couldn't remember his name, climbed into our boat lugging a red plastic fuel tank with them.

"A'ight," Kyle said. "Let's get this hooked up, see if it fixes things."

"I hope it does," Ian said nervously.

I hoped so too. Despite what Ian said, if we got caught, I would insist on taking the blame. This was entirely my fault.

Mont mentioned something about grabbing some tools and ducked into his cabin. Kyle and his friend set the tank down on the deck of the boat. Kyle said, "Robbie, grab the Teflon tape, will you?"

Robbie! That was his name.

As Robbie walked past me, he ran his eyes up and down my body. He looked at Ian, then back to me, and he whispered in my ear. "You get around, little chick. Kudos."

I shook my head and moved to the front by Ian. Kyle may have been "rugged," but Robbie was disgusting.

"You know these guys?" Ian asked.

"Not at all," I said, glad it was mostly true.

Once Robbie retrieved the tape, he and Kyle leaned over the tank, talking in quiet voices while they worked. After a while, Robbie stood up and reached into Mont's boat for a rag. His foot caught on my backpack.

"Oops. Sorry." He picked it up and handed it to me. It was still open, and a flipper popped out. "Hey, what have you got here?"

"That's mine." I reached for it, but he dangled it out of my reach. "Give it back."

"Yours?" He narrowed his eyes in consideration. "Interesting. Hey, Kyle, take a look at this." He yanked the skin out of the bag, dropped the bag to the floor, and tossed the skin to his friend. He then stood between Kyle and I while Kyle pawed at it, twisting it around, sticking his hands inside of it.

My stomach churned, and I tried to push past Robbie. He blocked me. Ian grabbed my arm and pulled me back beside him.

"Don't." Ian's fingers pinched tightly around my bicep.

Robbie watched us, his knees bent like a dog about to attack. "That's smart," he said to Ian. "You don't want your little pet to get hurt."

Pet?

"Hey!" Ian snapped at him. "You don't talk like that to her."

Robbie straightened up and took a step forward. I may have thought Jamie could win in a fight with him, but I doubted Ian could. Though I really didn't want to find out.

"Mont!" I screamed.

"Yeah?" Mont popped out of his cabin, a wrench and a set of pliers in his hands. He took in the scene: Ian and I backed up against the dash, gripping each other, Robbie inching closer to us, and Kyle behind him, clutching my skin like he knew exactly what it was. Mont focused on Kyle and raised his eyebrow. "Is that . . ." He dropped his arms. The tools clunked to the floor.

"Yep. No wonder we couldn't find it. She had it buried somewhere from the looks of it." He indicated my backpack which was covered in mud stains.

"Wait? Find it?" They were looking for it?

"Yep," Kyle said, balling up my skin like a used rag and tossing it into Mont's boat. "Mont told me he didn't know what I was talking about, but I heard you in that store. Now, come on." He grabbed me by the waist and attempted to toss me into Mont's boat. I say "attempted," because the second he put his hand on me, I kicked him in the crotch. "Hey!" He grabbed my arms and twisted them behind my back.

"Get off her!" Ian must've hit the guy, because Kyle let me go long enough to get my arms free. I turned around to see Robbie drop a fire extinguisher on top of Ian's head.

Ian crumpled to the deck.

"What the hell?" I screamed.

Ian lay on his side, unconscious. *Please let him just be unconscious.*

"Robbie!" Mont barked.

"There's only one way to do things." Robbie pointed his finger at Mont. "And clearly, your way didn't work. This time I'm taking care of it." He twisted me around, pinning my arms around my waist. "Now you listen good." His breath was hot in my ear and reeked of month-old cigarettes. "We're gonna take you and that skin of yours, and we're going to go look for something. If you help us, we won't dump your rich boy overboard. And if you don't . . ." His fists jammed into my ribcage, putting a period on the threat.

Tears streamed down my face. I looked to the one person who might be able to explain what was happening. "Mont?"

He clutched my seal skin to his chest. He looked like he might cry too. "I'm sorry. This wasn't supposed to happen. Your grandma should've given them the skin. Nothin' would've happened to her if she'd just given them the skin."

"So, Mr. Flannigan didn't—"

"Shut up!" Robbie's words rumbled against my back. "What do you think you're doing?" he said to Mont.

"She has a right to know what happened to her kin. Both human and not."

"Ain't nothing human about her or those other girls. You know it just as well as I do!" His fists tightened against my chest, and I fought to breathe.

"Mont, please!"

"Robbie! You let her go!" Mont dropped my skin into his boat and lifted a stiff leg over the side, his face pinched up with the effort.

Robbie shoved me against the dash. My head cracked against the windshield, and I slid to the floor. My vision doubled. I blinked, trying to put it all back into one image.

While Kyle worked to untie the ropes, Robbie went for Mont. He pounded his fist into Mont's jaw, then pushed him back into the fishing boat. I was next. He lifted me up like a rag doll and dumped me in beside Mont. My head felt like it was splitting open, and I didn't have the strength to sit up.

"Kyle, we gotta go. Now!"

"Yep." Kyle and Robbie hopped into Mont's boat, leaving Ian on the floor of the *Speedy Little Devil*. Soon, I heard the engine rumble beneath me, and my body rocked as we took off. The movement brought bile up into my throat.

Mont lay beside me, staring at me with glassy blue eyes.

I didn't need a courage builder to ask this question. I only needed my pain. "Why?"

# Chapter Twenty-Five

"Selkies." Mont coughed. A thin line of blood trickled from his mouth that he didn't wipe away. "All my life I ain't never seen nothin' but hate and cruelty come from them. They tortured me, kept me hostage and gnawed on my leg til I couldn't walk straight."

"So . . . so that story was real? And you're doing this for revenge?"

"Them boys approached me with a plan to get some money, and with the store going belly up, I couldn't turn it down. No one was supposed to die. I'm not cruel like them selkies."

"They're not cruel either, Mont."

"Think about your boat accident. They stole you and left your grandpa to die. Least that's what your momma always said."

"But, they're not . . . They wouldn't . . ." But the thing was, I didn't know much about selkies at all. I didn't know the whole truth of the accident. I'd only been three at the time, and no one knew exactly what happened to Grandpa Colm. Maybe someone could have prevented it. Maybe they tried and failed. I might never know for sure. With a splitting headache and drifting thoughts, I let it go for now.

The boat started to rock, and I knew we'd left the bay behind, entering the much rougher waters of the Pacific. I slipped an inch or two across the deck and reached for a chair leg to steady myself.

Mont grabbed my hand instead. "Please. I didn't know before, what they did to your grandma. I'm so sorry."

I squeezed his fingers. Maybe to reassure him. Or maybe I was just holding on. "But, Mont, that doesn't make it okay."

"No," he agreed. "None of this is okay." His eyes watered, and he seemed so fragile just lying there.

"Hey!" Robbie toed me in the ribs. "Get up. I need you to show me something." He grabbed my upper arm and pulled me to my feet, nearly yanking my arm out of the socket. I stumbled, my feet refusing to work right and my head screaming in pain.

"You let her go!" Mont called from the deck, but there wasn't anything he could do. He couldn't even sit up.

Robbie forced me over to the edge of the boat, holding me up by the shoulders. The waves slapped the side, and I had to hold on to keep my balance. We were sitting idle about a mile or so from the coastline. In front of us were a few nicer houses, and a whole lot of trees. To the far left, I saw the pier where Jamie kissed me, and his tiny cabin, barely visible through the forest.

Robbie shook me, and for a second, my vision doubled again. My knees wobbled beneath me. I tightened my grip on the railing to stop my legs from crumpling altogether. "Where are they?"

So, that's why they'd brought me along. Bridget must have left some clue in her note as to their location, but they didn't know exactly where. "How should I know?" My words came out in a slur.

"From what Mont said, they don't leave their own behind."

I really wished my head would stop spinning, so I could kick him or . . . something. For all the good it would do. I was still in the middle of the water. "Well, they did."

"You're lying!" One arm snaked around my throat, so tight. Painful.

My lips pressed together and trembled. A whimper escaped from between them.

"Cool it!" Kyle appeared beside us. "Let me talk to her. Can't you see she can barely stand?" He sounded nicer than Robbie, but only just.

"Whatever." Robbie released his grip on me, and I slumped against Kyle. Not really my first choice, but between him and the water, I'd choose him.

He led me to the captain's chair and helped me onto it. The motion of the boat—or maybe just the motion inside my head—made me grab hold of the seat's edges.

"Hey, you're all right," Kyle murmured. "Go on. Take a minute."

"I . . . I need . . ." My mommy. A doctor. Someone. I fell against the seat back, and my eyes slid shut.

"Hey." Kyle tapped my cheeks. "Stay with me. You're gonna be okay. We just need some information from you." He smoothed some hair off my forehead and cupped my face with both hands. I opened my eyes. He was very close and seemed almost kind. "Now, you want to help us, don't you? So we can get you home?"

"Home?" That seemed so far away.

"Aileen." He stroked my hair. "Come on, sweetie."

"Sweetie?" He didn't have the right to call me that. Only my dad. A sob tore up out of my throat. I wanted my Daddy. "Was that what you called Bridget too? Before you . . ." I sucked in a painful breath. It had to fight to get through the choking tears. "She's sick. And the others are gone because of you."

"No. No," he insisted. "I didn't do any of it. It wasn't me."

"Him then." I cut my eyes over to Robbie who was pacing back and forth behind Kyle, his shoulders scrunched up, his movements manic. Every now and then, he'd pause to eye my pelt, which lay on the floor near Mont. "It doesn't matter. You're just as guilty as he is. It's just as sickening." I worked up a hunk of spit and flung it in his face.

Kyle rocked back on his heels and swiped the back of his hand across the spit. He didn't look so nice anymore. "Robbie."

Robbie broke out of his pattern and stomped over to me. "You're done." He yanked me out of the chair, but I fell to my hands and knees. My eye focused on something sharp and pointy, two inches from my hand.

I grabbed the pliers Mont had dropped, and when Robbie bent over to pull me up, I rolled onto my back and nailed him in the head. The pointy ends tore across his forehead. Blood poured into his eyes.

"Aggh! Bitch!" He clutched his head and fell on top of me, pinning me to the deck. I hit him again, this time in the arm.

"Get off of me." I pulled my arm back a third time, but Kyle had pulled Robbie away by then. Robbie lay in a ball much like Ian when we'd left him. *Oh God, Ian!* Kyle lifted me to my feet. I tried to hit him, but he blocked me, twisted my arm until I was forced to drop the pliers. But I wasn't going down this time. I kneed him again, and when he doubled over, I retrieved my pelt from the floor.

Kyle stumbled toward me. I ran for the side, unsure what the plan was from there. It didn't matter, because he caught my shoulder, yanking me around to face him and pinning me against the railing with my arms twisted behind my back.

"That's mine," he said. "You aren't going anywhere with it."

I struggled to break free. His fingers pressed bruises into my arms. Yellow splotches popped in front of my eyes. "Go to hell!"

"I already been there, sweetie. And the money I get from that skin will buy my way out." He leaned in close enough for me to smell the motor oil on his skin.

My back arched backwards; my lower spine pressed painfully against the railing. I heard the sound of splintering wood, and I slipped backwards even further. My head hung upside down over the churning water. My brain throbbed in protest.

"Get off me!" I kicked, hard. I wasn't sure what I connected with, but it hurt him. He let go. Without his weight holding me down, my feet left the deck, and since my arms were still pinned behind me, I had no way to grab hold of anything. My body tilted backwards and my legs kept going, right over my head and straight into the water below. The pelt and part of the railing came with me. The small section of wood was enough to keep me afloat. I tried to kick away, but the waves kept smacking me in my face, pushing me back toward the boat.

Kyle dove over the edge. I'd put about ten feet between us, but he could swim! He was on me within seconds, ripping the pelt from my hands.

"No!" I screamed, but it was too late. He was already swimming back to the boat, and I was left to the unforgiving ocean, clutching a hunk of wood and wondering how long it would be before the water claimed me for good. "No." My eyes stung with salt. The world blurred around me as the tears streamed down my face and were swallowed up by the waves. One, two, three, four, five, six, seven . . .

The water around me exploded. At least two dozen seals shot to the surface, all of them aiming toward Kyle. His eyes grew big as Frisbees and he paddled furiously, trying to reach the boat. He didn't make it. At all.

His arms flailed as he went under. His screams were covered by the loud seal barks, and from that moment on, all I could see was a frenzy of tails and fins, tearing through the water and sending sprays up higher than the boat. When the sprays of water became tinged with red, I looked away.

Soon after, the cries died down, but I kept my head turned. The cold crept under my skin, and I began to shiver. My fingers slipped from the railing. Just then, a sleek, brown seal popped up beside me and wedged his head under my arm. My pelt was pinched between his teeth. I slipped my other arm around him, and he pulled me to shore.

# Chapter Twenty-Six

As soon as we reached land, Jamie suggested I transform into my seal skin. He helped me, and the two us rested on the beach while I healed. In the hour or so it took for me to recover, a lot of things happened: Mont told Mr. Flannigan where he could find Deirdre and Bridget's pelt, the police were called, and Mont confessed to having knowledge of both Deirdre and Fee's death. Robbie, on the other hand, chose to remain silent. Both were taken away to the local station for booking, while only bits and pieces of Kyle were ever found. My mom suggested his death had been caused by a shark. I'd been lucky to escape, and the news called me a miracle child.

At the same time the police were called, an ambulance boat was dispatched for Ian. He'd been knocked unconscious, but was otherwise fine. What his dad would do to him, well, that was another story. I still planned to speak to Mr. Glenn to see if I could reduce the punishment, claiming that, "Hey, we caught the bad guys. Doesn't that count for something?"

My mother was *not* furious, which was surprising to say the least. Oh, we talked, a lot, and she kept me home for two weeks under the guise that I still needed to heal, but I think she was starting to ease up. She understood I wasn't a little girl anymore, and I was going to make mistakes. Huge ones, in fact. But she wanted to experiment with a little trust. I think a lot of it had to do with the fact that I told her I didn't know what to think about selkies anymore. For now, my skin could stay hidden in the attic until I figured out what I wanted to do. She said she understood, and for the most part left me alone, because she knew that's what I needed.

On my fourth day home, a skinny, bald man with wire rimmed glasses knocked on our door. He introduced himself as Rod Thornton, Mr. Glenn's friend from a "special" department within the government. He didn't clarify beyond that, but I wouldn't have been surprised if he also had details of what was hidden at Area 51.

"Can I speak with Mr. Shay, please?" he asked me.

I led him into the kitchen—the living room was still off limits as far as I was concerned—and my family and I sat with him around our kitchen table.

"Isaac said this all belonged to your family." Mr. Thornton handed my dad a check.

I leaned across the table to see the computer printed number and nearly fell over at the large amount of zeros following that six. "Dad, you know what this means, right?"

His face lit up and I swore he was about to burst into song, but surprisingly, he held himself in check as he addressed our guest. "Thank you. This means a great deal to us."

Mr. Thornton pushed his glasses back up his nose and smiled. "You know, there might be more work for you. If you're interested." He handed over a card which my dad tucked behind a magnet on our refrigerator.

Dad said, "I'll be in touch." Mom cleared her throat and Dad amended his statement. "That is, after I consult with my family."

"Of course." Mr. Thornton closed the latch on his briefcase and stood up, but before he could leave, I stopped him.

"Can I ask you a question?"

He paused, giving me his full attention. "Sure."

"The Flannigans wouldn't cooperate with the police after Deirdre's death, and they never called anyone about Bridget. How did you and Mr. Glenn know what was going on?"

A touch of humor played across his face and settled into a twinkle at the corner of his eye. "Well, most of that family chooses to remain hidden, but there are one or two who seek out my help every now and then. I do my best to oblige."

"So you have an informant in their family? Who is it?" Jamie's uncle? His mom?

"I'm afraid I wouldn't keep my job very long if I revealed my sources." He pushed his chair under the table and scooted past me, heading for the door. "But who knows?" He shot a wink back at me. "Maybe you'll figure it out for yourself one day."

Not the answer I wanted to hear, but it looked like my curiosity would have to wait. "Well, thanks for everything."

"Yes, thank you." My mom escorted Mr. Thornton out, but as soon as he had stepped off the front porch, she turned around, dragged Dad into their bedroom, and shut the door. I listened for a minute, long enough to hear Mom ask why she hadn't known about this "work," but I was too happy to worry about their fight. I skipped into my bedroom, knowing we had the money to save the store, and soon we'd be celebrating.

I sat down in my window seat with legs crossed, touched my fingers to the window, and watched the sunset. Every color showed up that night. I longed to paint it, but I wouldn't have been able to do it justice, not even with my best acrylics. I didn't want to take my eyes off it anyway.

Once the sun had fully disappeared, my eyes slid across the water. It was a fairly calm night, but there was one thing breaking the surface. The seal ducked under and resurfaced several times, watching me, until I opened my window and stepped out onto the sand.

He swam parallel to the shore. I walked down the beach, following him until we both reached the cave we'd transformed in that day. By the time I stepped in, he was sitting on the floor as Jamie, and his seal skin was lying beside him.

"Where's your skin?" he asked.

"I don't really feel like going for a swim. I need some time to—"

"I'm not talking about a swim." He jumped to his feet and came over to face me. He stood so close, and my heartbeat reminded me of how deeply I'd fallen for him before everything happened. "I'm talking about you coming with me. For good." He cupped my face in his palms. "You belong with us. You always have."

"What? No!" I said as I lifted my hands to his chest and pushed against him. He grabbed my fists in his before I could pull completely away.

"Please. It's not safe here."

"It's as safe as it's ever gonna be. Mont and Robbie are in jail. Kyle's dead. Or did you forget that?" Sure, Kyle was guilty as sin, but now Jamie had blood on his hands too. Did that makes things any better? I didn't know.

Jamie hung his head and sighed. "Aileen, what do you want me to do? How do I fix this?" I broke our gaze choosing to focus on his collar bone instead of his eyes. Was he offering to fix things because he felt bad or because he knew it bothered me? There was a world of difference between the two. "Please tell me. I want you with me."

"Jamie, even if you could fix it, you know I can't take off and—"

"Please." He slid his hands behind my head tangling his fingers in my hair and pressing his forehead against mine. Not fair. I could never resist him when he was that close. I closed my eyes and settled against him. "You need to be with someone who can protect you, keep you close, keep you hidden."

And then my eyes popped open, remembering the one other time his family had hidden me, and the questions that had gone unanswered for too long. "When I was little, your family watched over me when I got lost in that storm. Ian said your dad told Fee that she would regret taking me from them. They never intended to give me back, did they? Not until Fee came to get me."

Jamie released me and took a step back, stuffing his hands in his pockets. He didn't need to answer after that, but he did anyway. "No, but they made a deal with your grandmother. She said she would take you home, and when you got older, she'd make sure you had the choice."

"What if I don't know what to choose?"

"Of course you know what to choose. You've told me the ocean calls to you."

"I'm only sixteen. I've got two more years of school and then college. I don't want to give that up. And I can't leave my family. Not after . . ." I still couldn't talk about it. Maybe one day I would be able to, but not now. And running away from it wasn't the answer.

He came back to me, wrapping his arms around me and holding me close. I let him. "I don't want to leave you behind, and my dad doesn't want me to keep coming back here."

"About that," I whispered against his shoulder. If he was finally telling me the whole truth, there was more I needed to ask. "You said you and your dad stuck around because you had things to do. Was I one of those things?"

He stayed quiet. Again his silence screamed louder than any words.

As more and more pieces clicked into place, I could feel my blood heating up. "What about when you took me to the island?"

"I realized my dad was right. It was our duty to protect you."

I wiggled out of his arms and backed up against the wall of the cave. What had he done? What had I let him do? He reached for me with one hand, and I knocked it out of the air. I felt dizzy. I clutched the cave wall for support.

"Aileen, please."

"You. Kidnapped. Me. And then you left me!"

"I'm sorry. When I got back, the police were at your house, and my dad said we had to go. They thought he did it."

"So what kept you from swimming out to get me? You're a freaking seal!"

"I *did* come back. As soon as the storm was over, I swam out there, but you were gone!"

"You . . . you did?"

"Yes. I was gonna take you home. My dad was wrong to force you to come with us. You should have a choice, just like your grandma wanted."

"Oh," I said, because what else was there to say. Nothing had actually changed. He had sided against his dad, but he was still asking me to go with him. He had come back for me, twice, but what did it matter when he was leaving for good?

"I guess you're not choosing me."

"How can I?"

Jamie walked out of the cave until he was ankle deep in the water.

I let him stay out there longer than I probably should have, but he stayed frozen for several long moments, so I did too. Eventually, I moved up beside him, both of us facing the horizon. A small sliver of moon reflected low on the water. "It's not you. I hope you understand that."

"It's fine." Though his tone made me wonder if it really was. "Do you think you'll ever change your mind?"

I was a sixteen year old girl. I changed my mind twenty five times a day about everything from clothes to music to bangs or no bangs. Anything was possible. "I might."

"Then I'll come back, even if my dad doesn't like it."

"When?"

"Whenever I can." He moved in front of me. He touched his fingers to my cheek. "I really do care about you."

"I know," I said. "But . . ."

"But what?"

But . . . I didn't know. Was it fair for him to ask me to wait, leaving me no idea where he was or when he'd be back. And even when he did come back, it would only be stolen moments until I decided to leave everything behind and go with him permanently. Did I want that kind of relationship at sixteen, no matter how incredible he made me feel? I reached up and caught a strand of his hair between two of my fingers. During our first walk on the beach, I had imagined a future for us. Was that even possible? "Jamie, I don't—"

He put his finger on my lips sealing them. He must have known what I was gonna say, because he gave me a way out. "Don't answer me now. Just say, 'I'll see you later.'" Then he pressed his lips to mine for a long minute.

When he stopped, he picked up his seal skin, and was gone, leaving me with four unspoken words on my lips. But whether they were "I'll see you later," or "I can't do this," I didn't know.

# Chapter Twenty-Seven

When Dad went back to work, he asked me to come with him. Without Mont, there would be a lot more to do, especially since we'd have to mark all the clearance stuff back to full price. I had no problem doing it, knowing with the check we got, we weren't going anywhere for a long time.

I followed Dad into the store. He had a brilliant smile and cherry, red cheeks, and was singing. "Sailing, sailing over the bounding Main."

I joined in, belting the notes at the top of my lungs, as I ripped the "Going Out of Business" sign from the store window.

Dad turned around, and with a playful wink, he said, "You'll want to leave that up there."

My good mood instantly vanished. He couldn't possibly be saying that, could he? "What? No! I thought we—"

Still smiling, Dad threw his arm around me and dragged me into the storeroom. "No arguing until I show you what's in here."

I stumbled after him, not arguing. But that didn't mean I couldn't register my protest in some other way. As soon as he released me, I stood glaring at him with my arms crossed.

He pulled Ben's contract from a manila envelope on the desk, and flipped to a section at the back, pointing to the page like he was proud of it. "Ben and I talked last week, and he added this as a condition of the sale."

I didn't want to look at it for fear I might go blind from those horrible words. But when Dad elbowed me, I begrudgingly scanned over the legalese until my eyes caught on my name. "Terms: Buyer agrees to provide a wall space equal or greater to 10' x 20' within Seal Bay Traders for Aileen Shay solely for the purposes of selling her wares. This term shall be in effect until such time as Miss Shay terminates the contract or Seal Bay Traders closes, whichever comes first." I looked to my dad. "What does that mean?"

"Apparently, he has a degree in contemporary art, and he was really impressed with a certain local artist. Looks like you're still in business, even if I'm not."

I threw the contract on the table. "But I don't want to be in business with him. We have the money to keep the store. Why are you doing this?"

"Because Seal Bay Traders is being built whether we like it or not, and there is no way we can compete with them. I'm not sinking the reward money into a store that has no future. It's going into a college fund for you."

"I've got a college fund! That's why I sell the paintings."

Dad sat down on the top of a small filing cabinet, so he was eye level with me. His face was deadly serious. "When is the last time you put money into that fund instead of giving it to me?"

"I . . . um . . ." I searched for a date that would prove my point. I wanted to say a couple of months ago, but the truth was I didn't remember. It had probably been a lot longer than that.

He took my hands. His worn, calloused fingers felt strong against mine. "Sweetie, I should have never taken money from you to begin with. It wasn't fair. The store was going to close. It was only a matter of time, and there is nothing you could have done to stop it."

"But . . ." I looked around the storeroom. I'd spent so many afternoons here. It was hidden now, but I could still picture the ocean life mural I'd penciled in across the back wall when I was ten.

Dad had helped, drawing little stick figure fish and blocky lines of seaweed. "You love this store."

"But I love fishing even more." The corners of his mouth crinkled up in a smile, and I knew there was something else he hadn't told me.

"Dad?"

"Your mom and I have talked a lot about this, and we think it's time I start up my fishing business again. The money I get from selling the store will be enough to buy a new boat and get some advertising out there. And we'll even have a little bit left over."

"Mom agreed to that?"

"Well, not at first, but she understands." Dad chucked me under my chin. "You're not the only one who hears the call of the sea."

Dad's first passion had always been the sea. He'd been a fisherman since before he met my mom, and it's what eventually brought them together. I'd always thought the store filled whatever hole left behind from selling his boat. But what if it hadn't? What if he was just better than me at hiding his sadness. Plus, if Dad had a boat again, I could go out in the water, legitimately. "Can I help? I could be your first mate."

"That, I'm afraid is still up to your mom."

"Of course." That was a hurdle for another day. He pulled me into a tight hug. I snuggled my head against his shoulder, and the frustration I'd felt since he showed me the contract began to fade. Maybe this would work. At the very least, Dad seemed happy, and that was all I really wanted.

# Chapter Twenty-Eight

I sat on my rock, staring out into the ocean. I had a lot of paintings to finish for the Seal Bay Traders grand opening in the fall, but I didn't feel like tackling that yet. Summer didn't last too long, and in another month, I wouldn't be able to sit out there without bundling up. It didn't mean I wouldn't do it, it just meant more hassle.

"You're not still pining, are you?" Mae's voice sounded from behind me. She squeaked as she waded through the shallow water to get to me. The cold water had never bothered me as much as it had her, and now I had a guess as to why.

"Not really." It had been over a month, and despite Jamie's promise to come back, I'd seen no sign of him, heard nothing from him. Still, I spent time watching the water every day. Maybe I was looking for him, or maybe I was just trying to understand who I was, and what future lay before me.

"Don't lie to me. You are," she said as she climbed onto the rock beside me. She had an oversized windbreaker on, and she pulled her legs up inside it to hide from the chills the water had given her. "I don't get it. It's not like you haven't had other offers."

I gave her a noncommittal shrug. I liked Ian. I really did. But could Ian ever understand me the way Jamie did?

"Well, if you insist on mooning over him, it is my duty as your BFF to moon with you." She scooted closer to me on the rock, which was a little difficult considering she was still bundled inside her jacket, and slung her arm over my shoulders. I rested my head against her, and the two of us stared out to the horizon. Although I didn't expect to sit there long. Patience had never been her strongest suit.

True to form, Mae only waited a minute or two before breaking the silence. "You know, he's probably not going to come back tonight."

"No," I agreed.

"In fact," she said thoughtfully, "he probably won't be back this week."

I looked up at her with one eyebrow raised. "What are you getting at?"

She flashed me her most innocent smile, and said, "I'm just saying I think you have time for a 7up float. Or two."

"With who?" I asked suspiciously.

"Me."

"And?"

"And . . . when school starts, you'll kill me for letting you waste your whole summer. So, get your pathetic butt off that rock and stop worrying about who may or may not be there."

"You mean the boys?" I asked.

"I don't know who you're talking about," she said innocently as she jumped up from the rock and dashed through the water.

I chased after her, laughing. "Tell me."

"No!"

"Yes!" I kicked a spray of water in her direction.

"No!" she shrieked.

We were both still arguing (and giggling) when we got into her car and headed off toward the diner to meet Ian and Steven.

When I got home, Mom was sitting on the couch, waiting for me with an open UPS box beside her.

"What's that?" I asked.

She handed it to me, and I peeked inside, hoping for some new photo paper for my printer or one of the ink cartridges I was always running out of, but when I saw the black, rubbery fabric, I squealed. "No way!"

A reluctant grin spread across her face. "Yes, way. Go put it on before I change my mind."

I pulled out my brand new wet suit, and stared at it, still not believing it was right there in my hands. That's when I noticed there was another one sitting beside her on the couch. "What made you change your mind?"

"You," she said quietly. "You and I are alike in so many ways. That's why I kept so many things from you. I thought it wouldn't matter. I thought if you were ever given the choice, you would come to the same decision I did. To give up the ocean, because in the end, it's just not worth it. If I had been you, I wouldn't have set foot on that beach after everything that happened. Yet you still go out there every day, staring at the water like it's speaking to you. For all I know, it is."

I nodded. I'd always felt like the waves were spilling secrets just for me. A lot of things had changed in the past weeks, but that hadn't been one of them.

"And I figured, you're going to face some big choices in the next few years. The least I can do is teach you what I can. It's my job to give you the tools to make the smart decisions, and back up plans for the not so smart ones. I haven't been too good with that, and I'm sorry."

It was the closest we'd come to talking about the night on Mont's boat. I figured it had been too painful for her to think about Fee, but now I saw it had just as much to do with her fear of losing me. Maybe more so. I ripped the tags off of my wetsuit. "I'll meet you out back in five."

Mom stood in waist deep water, her hands on my hips as I struggled to paddle.

"Loosen up," she said. "Lengthen your arms. Pull yourself through the water."

I kicked, probably a lot harder than I needed to, but I moved a little bit. Mom let go, and then I started to sink. Before I inhaled any water, I planted my feet on the sandy bottom and glared at my mom. "Don't do that!"

"Relax. It's salt water. Your body wants to float. Let it."

"Fine, but don't let go of me."

"I won't," she promised. "Not until you're ready."

I took a deep breath, willing my muscles to relax, and eased back onto my stomach. She was right. When I stopped struggling, it became a little easier. I stretched out my arms, cupped my hands, and straightened my knees. "Okay, I'm ready."

"All right then. One. Two. Three!"

She let go, and for the first time on my own, I kicked and paddled. Okay, it was still more flailing than paddling, but the point was, I wasn't gulping water, and I wasn't sinking. The ocean was holding me up, just like it always promised it would. And whether I chose to be a part of it, or simply enjoy the view, the water would always be there for me, waiting to speak or just to listen.

# Acknowledgements

The first people I absolutely must thank are my critique partners, Dianne K. Salerni and Amy Christine Parker. Dianne helped me build my story chapter by chapter. Without her, several characters wouldn't exist, including Ian who she kept insisting had a purpose. Amy gave me wonderful advice on several different drafts and introduced me to the writing community in Orlando.

Thank you also to my beta readers: Marcy Hatch, Serena Kaylor, and Jennifer Manley. Each one of these ladies inspired me in different ways.

Finally, I am grateful to my family: Scott, for understanding that Monday nights are my writing nights, and my son, whose smiles light up my day.

# Thank You For Reading

# About The Author

**Krystalyn Drown** has spent the past thirteen years working at Walt Disney World in a variety of roles: entertainer, talent coordinator, and character captain. Her degree in theatre as well as many, many hours spent in a dance studio, helped with her job there.

Her various other day jobs have included working at Sea World in zoology, as an elementary teacher, and currently as a support technician for a website. In the evenings, she does mad writing challenges with her sister, who is also an author.

Krystalyn lives near Orlando, Florida with her husband, son, a were cat, and a Yorkie with a Napoleon complex.

**Ever, by Jessa Russo**

Seventeen-year-old Ever's love life has been on hold for the past two years. She's secretly in love with her best friend Frankie, and he's completely oblivious. Of course, it doesn't help that he's dead, and waking up to his ghost every day has made moving on nearly impossible.

Frustrated and desperate for something real, Ever finds herself falling for her hot new neighbor Toby. His relaxed confidence is irresistible, and not just Ever knows it. But falling for Toby comes with a price that throws Ever's life into a whirlwind of chaos and drama. More than hearts are on the line, and more than Ever will suffer.

**18 Things, by Jamie Ayres**

A young girl struggles to live again after a lightning strike kills the best friend she was secretly in love with.

Her therapist suggests she write a life list of eighteen things to complete the year of her eighteenth birthday, sending her and her friends, including the new hottie in town, on an unexpected journey they'll never forget.

As she crosses each item off her list, she must risk her own heart, but if she fails, she risks losing herself and her true soul-mate forever

**Fade, by A.K. Morgen**

When Arionna Jacobs loses her mother in a tragic accident, her world is turned upside down. She's forced to leave her old life behind and move in with her father. Dace Matthews, a teaching assistant at her new college, is torn in two, unable to communicate with the feral wolf caged inside him. When they meet, everything they thought they knew about life unravels. Their meeting sets an ancient Norse prophesy of destruction in motion, and what destiny has in store for them is bigger than either could have ever imagined. Unless they learn to trust themselves and one another, they may never resolve the mystery surrounding who they are to one another, and what that means for the world.

**Wilde's Fire, by Krystal Wade**

Katriona Wilde has never wondered what it would feel like to have everything she's ever known and loved ripped away, but she is about to find out: her entire life has been a lie, and those closest to her have betrayed her. What's worse, she has no control over her new future, full of magic and horrors from which nightmares are made. Will Kate discover and learn to control who she really is in time to save the ones she loves, or will all be lost?

## The Gathering Darkness, by Lisa Collicutt

They say "third time's the charm", and for sixteen-year-old Brooke Day, they had better be right. She's been here before, twice in fact, and an evil demon-witch wants her dead a third time.

When Brooke is forced to leave Boston for the small town of Deadwich, she thinks her life is over. Before long, her new friends start acting strange-downright evil. But worse than that, nightmares she's had her whole life become reality. Enter Marcus Knight; popular, hot, and the only person Brooke can trust. Brooke and Marcus unravel the secrets of her past, which reveals the key to her future.

## Death By Chocolate, by Johanna Pitcairn

At seventeen years old, Julie deals with more problems than most teenagers her age. A runaway, she quickly ends up homeless and broke. When an old Gypsy woman offers to read her future in exchange for a meal, the challenge sounds like a dare. The tarot cards reveal a great destiny, and a perilous journey – and a red heart shaped box of chocolates melts reality and fantasy into one never ending nightmare where failure equals death.

Julie wakes up in an unwelcoming world filled with danger. Demons of a long forgotten past haunt her dreams and seek revenge for something she doesn't remember. Will Julie accept the truth to survive?

CPSIA information can be obtained at www.ICGtesting.com
Printed in the USA
BVOW07s1745020214

343461BV00001B/44/P